Salomé

Salomé

A Novel

PATTI RUTKA

RESOURCE *Publications* • Eugene, Oregon

SALOMÉ
A Novel

Resource Publications
An Imprint of Wipf and Stock Publishers
199 W. 8th Ave., Suite 3
Eugene, OR 97401
www.wipfandstock.com

ISBN 13: 978-1-60899-093-1

Manufactured in the U.S.A.

for Ima Orman

When women sit and interpret the bible, the actual stories may begin to take on different meanings.

Rabbi Elyse Goldstein

I have now a mind to describe Herod and his family, how it fared with them . . . and learn thence how unhappy they were.

Flavius Josephus

Acknowledgments

M ANY PEOPLE have been agents in helping me bring forth this ministry of *midrash*. It is with profound gratitude that I thank Dr. David Trobisch, gentleman and scholar, who has worn many hats for me: teacher, mentor, minister, provocateur, inspiration. You have taught me more than I could ever express my thanks for. You have also given me a great gift, and so I say, A story, A story!

To Dr. Ann Johnston, RSCJ, role model, thank you for being the *ruach* in the sails of my *midrash*. Your love of scripture infuses my inquiry. Thank you for teaching me to responsibly seek answers to the question, "Who *is* this Jesus?"

I am profoundly grateful to my editor, Ulrike Guthrie, who was right when she told me with a light in her eye that I wouldn't be happy without writing. Without your keen editorial sense and grounding reassurance this would not have come to pass; your experience is a treasure.

Thanks to Diane Farley and Christian Amondson and all the folks at Wipf and Stock, who have dealt so patiently with me and with such good guidance. Thanks also to Kristin Firth, whose combination of professionalism, sharp eye, and kind tongue made the copyediting process quite fun.

Thanks to Marissa Stam, Dorothy Barker, and the crew, as well as to Dr. Ali Abdulatif Ahmida for providing limitless encouragement and optimism, and John, for showing me the importance of showing up to write day by day.

Thank you to the Reverend Dr. Milton Ryder, Pastor Emeritus, for stepping up at the last minute, and for an early conversation with him which drew me down this life-giving path.

To the PPCS: you keep me afloat and balanced when I am not writing, and for this I am grateful.

And to my loving husband, Tom: your constancy sustains me in this, my pursuit; you have tolerated much. I get some of my best ideas from you. Your love and support mean more than the world to me.

1

67 CE

ERHAPS YOU have been jostled from dreams the way my mother woke me one roseat sky morning from a dream of chickens, feathers flying on the still dawn before the market's din began. I stretched and yawned as they fluttered and squawked away, leaving me in my own quiet world of youth and soft skin against the pallet's coarse linens. So I roused to the lower city of Machaerus east of the Dead Sea and relinquished the jumbled prism of my increasingly complicated adolescent dream world.

I rose and dipped my face in the clay bowl half-filled with tepid water from the night before. Dressing, I slipped a blue-dyed flax outer tunic around me, then my headdress, without which I could not appear in public, rustled into the central area that served as kitchen and sitting room together, found some flat bread and olives, and stuffed them in my mouth. Gathering up stylus, ink well, and my beloved but scuffed and marred tablet, I almost spilled ink into the leather pouch in which I carried my scribe's tools. My mother's eyes narrowed when I glanced quickly back at her, then she pursed her lips. She had been up before first light and looked worn even in the gentlest light of the early hour. Dipping my head, I went out from the cool stone cave that was our small dwelling in the poorer section of the city, into the familiar smells of donkey piss and rising dust as workers woke and groaned to their tasks.

As I walked I picked at my fingers. My palms sweated. Today I would meet the aging Queen Salomé in the fortress that had been built by Herod the Brutal in order to watch over the eastern frontier, occupied these last years by Roman filth; we had hopes the Jewish rebels would reclaim it soon. Salomé's reputation was not for kindness, though my knowledge—and that of everyone else to whom I spoke of her—was murky. But I was grateful because I needed the work, to help my father and mother buy food. Among the town's poor, we were relentlessly squeezed by wealthy landowners who came from outside of Israel to buy up land that had been in families for centuries, forcing farm people like we had been to move to the cities and towns.

I had been brought up in Machaerus, first, but had gone to Jerusalem to live with my mother's sister for my training as a scribe when I was nine. It was an unusual choice for a Jewish girl, since most scribes were Greek or Roman, but I had a talent for writing. The stay in Jerusalem made me question my parents' choice to live in Machaerus. Why my father had years ago chosen the dry, small town, hemmed in by tall ravines on three sides, I didn't know, unless it was for the work. Only on occasion now was I able to visit my parents and be struck anew by the poverty that pressed upon them. Our existence was as strangled and dry as the land surrounding us; taxes took up fifty percent of all of my family's income. Living at subsistence level, we breathed in both the stench of crucifixions as well as our own rage at being under the heel of our pagan oppressors.

At least my handwriting was beautiful. I had been well trained during my time in Jerusalem, and I hoped to impress the queen today. Breathing hard, I made my way up the steep laid limestone streets of Machaerus's northern end, now and then catching a glimpse of the citadel walls on the high plateau. The fortress seemed to press against the horizon, reaching higher for rain from the sky at the same time that it was anchored squatly to the harsh ground beneath it. As if locked in, its new inhabitants rarely mixed with the ordinary townspeople, though we whispered about them.

We whispered particularly about the queen. Secretive and inaccessible, people said she was. Still traveling frequently at her age, she had gained permission to visit the now decimated fortress of her youth after the Romans had destroyed it some twenty years ago. She had not been seen in these parts for years, not since she had married and moved to the north. Rumors spun that she had lost her beauty, that her face had fallen like some of the walls of the citadel, that she saw no one except those closest in her entourage and her three sons, and they only when she was heavily veiled and they heavy with wine.

Most of this I had learned from my cousin, Nathaniel, who still lived and worked in Jerusalem as a cook in the household of the wealthy and regal Greek widow Theophile, but he had only been able to give me wisps of information. It was he who had connected me with the scribal work to which I was headed this day, the work that could be known by none, not even my family. It was work on which I would start with the queen, the true author, but I would never see her after this beginning and I was to keep my peace. When I had asked my parents if I could come back to Machaerus and spend some time with them, my mother suspected I was doing something in violation of the Law. I had told her I could not reveal to whose employ and for what purpose I went, but I was old enough to keep quiet and expect my mother would let me alone about it: I was, after all, sixteen and unmarried. Perhaps the people occupying the palace had chosen me for the work because they knew that I did not have a husband or children to whom I would relate stories at night and that, despite my family's poverty, I had been well educated.

"She has work," was all my mother had said to my father. And my younger sisters and brothers, still at home, did not even know where it was I went, nor did they care, so long as there would be food at the end of the day. My father—well, he broke into one of his fits of spewing cough with the tiny flecks of blood that sometimes came, wiped his face on a rag, and nodded his head in assent. Nor did he care about the details; he was too exhausted. His religious inclinations had more to do with appearances than conviction, so he would not be especially bothered that I would be taking dictation in violation of the Law forbidding Jews to do so—unless someone else found out about it. I had balanced accounts, and copied some scrolls and the new codex-book form used primarily by the Yeshua-followers, the people called Christians by some. But as Jews we were not allowed to take dictation, unlike the Greeks and Romans; for some strange convoluted reason (it seemed to me), it was considered idolatrous. And of course Jewish women like me were not allowed to copy the sacred literature, though that had more to do with tradition and laws of purity. I would take what I could get, no matter how difficult the employer, and if I was in my cycle, well, then, I would simply go to the ritual bath for purification without alerting anyone about it.

Had he not come home each day so collapsed from his work at the olive presses, I would have asked my father's advice. Escaping the heat of the day, he worked in the underground rooms of the presses, but his back and ribs were nearly shattered from first pushing the large timber used to move the massive olive crusher stone. He then had to adjust the limestone blocks that would press down on the slurry to extract from them the oil that was a staple for us all. It was truly back-breaking labor, and for relief my mother could only put hot flax compresses on him at night. I wondered some days where his dreams took him when he slept fitfully. Doubtless to worlds different from mine.

My father, my dear wise *Abba*, would have been able to advise me about whether or not to take this odd work with a woman of such peculiar reputation. My mother I would not so easily ask, for her views were more limited, more confined to her own life in the town, and her life centered on her children. She had had little experience with the Romans and Greeks, considering we lived surrounded by them now. So I had realized I would have to turn to someone else for wisdom about the job offer.

When Nathaniel had come to me in Jerusalem and told me he had heard talk from his employer that the queen was writing something new and needed a discreet scribe, I quickly told him I could do it. He had told me he would speak about it to the head cook, the crooked crone who mixed stews and relationships alike, the woman who was his best informant at the widow Theophile's house. Three days later a small and ancient man, elegantly dressed in deep blue and green and gold-bordered robes but possessing bad teeth, had arrived at the door of my aunt's house.

My aunt, being a poor judge of character, had invited in the peacock-man with the rotted mouth as I stood just off her shoulder, curious. He tucked his chin down to the floor as he touched his hand to the mezuzah and daubed some oil on his thinning strands of hair combed across his scalp.

"My name is Obed," he said in a voice as incongruously raucous as the bird he resembled. I wondered how he had garnered favor with those whom he served. "I serve Queen Salomé. She has work for a scribe who will be able to travel with her and keep silence and not expect communication after the project is finished. Do you understand me? To speak of the work to anyone would result in unpleasant consequences. It would be good if you and I could speak alone," and here he bore hard black eyes at my aunt then looked over her shoulder directly at me. Unlike other men, he seemed to be uninterested in her form or mine, seeming to take into account only our expressions as he spoke.

"Surely you can speak of it to my aunt as well as me," I countered, not willing to be made the subject of inquiry in my own home.

He raised an eyebrow, then sucked air in through his remaining teeth. "Well. That lies with the queen. As do—ah, well," he muttered, intending to keep me out of his thoughts and whatever inner circle of knowledge he possessed of his mistress. He pointed at me, his breath coming in a small stale stream, as I blinked in its wash. "You would not want to lose your head over this matter."

So I had asked Nathaniel again for more information of the queen, because I was certain the differences between the way she lived and the way my family lived would present me with some etiquette situations that I would not want to violate. At first he told me only what we had already heard in the accounts from the Yeshua-followers, one that was being distributed at small, clandestine gatherings in houses and attributed to an author named Mark, and the other account more literary, though the author we had not heard of.

Nathaniel told me that one starlit evening in the beauty of her youth, before I had been born, Salomé had danced for Herod Antipas, tetrarch of Galilee, in the fortress at Machaerus above the Dead Sea. The evening of entertainment had been for his pleasure as well as his guests' in celebration of his birthday, and possibly was intended to stave off war by bringing together his high-ranking guests. Veiled and wrapped in bangles, in a mosaic-floored banquet room with splashing pools, fig trees, and vines, the young Salomé had performed so enticingly, so sensuously, that Herod, out of two desires—his own arousal, and the impulsive urge to impress his guests—had promised his stepdaughter anything. Lust growing beneath his robe, Herod frightened Salomé out of a childishness belying her blossoming form, so that she ran out to seek help from her mother Herodias, who was bathing in her quarters.

Political intrigue and revenge, rather than just a young girl's need for guidance, manipulated the remaining events of the night. By way of explanation, Nathaniel told me, Herodias's union with Herod had been declared by a popular prophet named John to be a stain on the soul of Israel. John, who had been baptizing people in the river near Machaerus so that God would forgive their sins, was unafraid to speak truth to power. He accused Herod of immorally even if legally marrying Herodias because Herodias had been the wife of Herod's half-brother, Philip; the violation was against Jewish tradition, everyone knew. Nonetheless Herodias could not forgive the exposure from John, so she, more brutal than her husband, rose naked from her steaming bath that night only to sink into more sin by ordering her shrinking daughter to ask for the head of John the Baptist on a silver platter.

Herod did have some respect for and fear of John as a holy man and a catalyst for people's passions, the very people who might rise up and dethrone Herod, so the tetrarch had imprisoned him in one of the cisterns at Machaerus rather than execute him, preferring to pretend the slight had not occurred. The longer John rotted in his dank prison the more Herod had seemingly freed himself of John's impudence. Herod's own impotence in the prophet's face seemed to grate more on his wife than on the Herod, however, so it was not surprising when Herodias stood and pronounced the request to her daughter. Who knew how long she had been soaking in her blood rage!

Thus, with one arm nailed by her mother's wrath, the other by Herod's lasciviousness, Salomé had to force her escape. She flew back to Herod. Nor did she neglect her mother's detail of the platter being silver; the princess's mother was exacting, and Salomé knew the price for omitting details her mother proscribed.

But even as Nathaniel told me the story, I was curious about its layers, sensing there was in it something as veiled as Salomé had been when she had started dancing that night. Why had Herodias involved her young daughter in her machinations? Why not demand John's head from Herod herself? I could only wonder at Herodias's and Salomé's relationship, and about what, to normal people, would have seemed a moral quandary in asking for the bloody execution. Could a daughter who had been commanded so, who had lived around a mother capable of such a rage-filled act, have escaped an inherited claim to such fury herself later in life? Like mother like daughter, the saying went. Did I really want this work?

Nathaniel had no information for me on these curiosities, as if they were beyond the native and local interest of his mind. Perhaps some of the curtains of mystery had been removed as the years had gone by, and if I were to work around the aging Queen Salomé I might learn more of the tale that had had such a gruesome end. Still, I was being called to work on a project about which I still knew nothing, and I needed to keep that in focus. As I sat with Nathaniel on that gray day in Jerusalem, the softness of the clouds battening down the sky like wads of cotton and tucking us in to the peace I had found in my aunt's household and the friendship I had formed with Nathaniel, I wondered to what scorching wilderness I was returning in Machaerus.

Machaerus had changed since Salomé's youth. Both Herodias and Herod had long since died, Herod having been exiled to Gaul some years ago and Herodias having accompanied him—some said to torture him further; this I knew from my aunt's political awareness. Though dead, Herod's reputation was as fresh as goat cheese packed at market. The Romans had bred across our land and expanded their occupation after Herod; they swamped our public areas, our bathing places, our worship, our senses. It wasn't just Jerusalem they desecrated; it was the whole of Israel, including Machaerus, like a bride and her younger sister having both been raped. Perhaps we kept alive our indignation at the Romans by remembering how Herod had been in bed with them as well. In any case, it was clear our dominators were not going to leave us anytime soon; our worst dreams no doubt came from dealing with them. Yet we held out hope that the zealot rebels might yet reclaim something for us. Queen Salomé was a reminder for me and for most Jews of the days that led up to the tense situation in which we now found ourselves. My father said war was just around the corner.

But for today in Machaerus I was consumed with what lay right before my eyes: the steep alleys woven with rat-tailed cats as they slunk through looking for vermin, the boney stone paths leading from my parents' house in the lower city up to the hunkering fortress that temporarily housed the queen. The odor of sweat from the Roman soldiers' heavy leather and metal armor, along with their horse crap, rose in a stinking steam throughout the town. As a rule they were hard, brutal men, physical in a way we Jews were not. I had often wondered what their women were like—we didn't see many of them here, and when they did pass through they were the wives of the higher-up Roman military, and therefore cultured, educated, and pagan. I believed them immodest in their clothing draped off their shoulders, exposing their skin, taking pride in the symbolism of the fabric and drapery of their clothing. Jews generally, and certainly of my standing, did not have any dealings with those women. Occasionally we would see them out parading their high hairstyles and finely wrought footwear, but as a rule we disdained and had little contact with them. Somewhat naively, I supposed, I wondered if the queen would have had many dealings with them. As it would turn out, she was far more culturally exposed than I could have imagined.

I made my way up toward the fortress, musing on all these thoughts, the heat of the day pressing in. Closer in my view now than it had ever been, the stone citadel rose up, imposing against the sky, blocking out views of the Dead Sea to the east as I approached. My first impression reinforced itself: thickset, it spread heavy across the ground, a weighty stronghold containing its occupants and repelling anyone on the exterior who would try to breach it. It seemed to quash the arid boney land beneath it, broadening its shoulders from the height on which it sat. And yet impotent, it couldn't balance out the expansive sky above nor the endless hills that wandered off to the horizon, running to the north and west in rivulets of dried-up wadis as if God had painted them into existence with a wavering finger, then dotted the landscape with the palace for emphasis.

Plucking from under my armpits my clothing moistened with exertion from the ascent, I made my way up the rampart that led like a tongue into the swallowing mouth of the receiving fort. Coming to an unimposing side entrance to which Obed had directed me, I passed a guard, explained who I was, and ducked down a cool dark corridor. As I continued on soundlessly, it bloomed into a sizeable, brightly lit courtyard. High up a few mourning doves nestled, cooing, and I waited as I had been instructed. They quieted, as if sensing my presence, and an eerie stillness sank into the space.

Then as from an underground cavern I heard children's laughter burbling in the distance. Soon a boy, whose hair had been goldened from days outside the confining walls of the courtyard, and a girl, whose laughter ran like spring freshets in the desert, came spilling into the courtyard. So alike were they in appearance that I stared. When the boy saw me he checked himself, and the girl's bouncing curls followed to see what he was looking at. I smiled, and the boy put fists on hips, facing me.

"You are?"

"I am here for the queen, as a scribe."

"For her Highness!" he corrected, pointing a finger at me. Then he began laughing and dropped his arm. He grabbed the girl and pulled her toward me, swinging her arm. She wriggled free of his grasp, and they both stood close to me, looking me up and down.

"I am Joachim, the son of Prince Aristobolus," he announced. "This is Meira, my sister."

"So very pleased to meet you, your Highnesses," I answered solemnly. "I am here to do scribal work for your grandmother, Salomé. Did you have a good journey from the north?"

"Granny is not quite right in her head today," said the little girl, ignoring my question as she came up closer to me to peer into my face. A beauty that, given a few more years, would surely stop a man's breath created around her an aura. Nor had the inherited good looks escaped her brother, and I imagined he would have his way with young women as he grew older. Particularly if he lived between Greek and Roman and Jewish cultures because the Greeks and Romans were so much more free in their habits than were we Jews.

I knelt down before Meira. "Not quite right in her head? What do you mean?" My curiosity, while quiet in this imposing new landscape, knew no constraints before the young girl.

In the dreamlike quality of a child's narrative, drawing with colorful clarity that skips over the connections and transitions that link a story, thereby making it intelligible, Meira came within a breath's feel of my face and spoke in a whisper, then reached her lips up to my ear.

"The days she dances with the red scarves are the days she's hardest to talk to. When she sits and bows her head with the blue scarves and the gold necklaces and cries, she's not as scary to play with. But on days like today her feet move on their own and she's very hard to talk to." I raised an eyebrow at her, looking earnestly into her young amber eyes. Ordinarily I would have let the comments go, knowing the child would not be the most reliable of commentators on an elderly woman with a tragic history stretching so far back, but something in her honest face left my mind to swirl anew around Salomé's story.

Our reverie was interrupted. A middle-aged woman with gnarled hands and wearing a bloodied apron came into the yard, planted her feet, and took in the scene between me and the children.

"Away! Go play in the courtyard, or with the birds. This young woman has work to do."

Scowling, Joachim again clasped Meira's hand and began to lead her out.

"You won't always be able to tell me what to do, Joanna," he complained.

"But for now I can, so go on with you. Leave us." Her scowl was enough to frighten most any young person, but apparently he was used to it and not impressed. Joanna brushed her rough hands on her apron. "They are so much work to travel with, but the queen insists," she said in exasperation, as the children flitted out into other sunlit areas of the intricately designed courtyards.

As the children exited to the west wing, the hot and red-faced Joanna brushed wisps of hair out of her eyes, looked me up and down, then sighed. "You have come on a difficult day, but there is nothing we can do about it. The queen has made clear she does not want to wait on her composition, so today you will begin. Come with me. I just hope this works," she muttered, as we moved at a healthy pace despite a lope in Joanna's gait. I needed to remember I was not here for my own inquisitiveness but for a task.

Joanna's fingers were blackened with some substance, her eyes careworn, but she remembered the intricacies of not just the passageways of the now-skeleton fortress, but the children's potential indiscretions, as well as her mistress's moods. I wondered again with trepidation whether the queen had a volatile temperament, and was about to ask. Surely it would have a bearing on my work. But as if attuned to every slight movement of my face, Joanna told me, "You ask no questions. You speak only when the queen speaks directly to you, and you keep your answers brief. You are hired to write, not engage in conversation. Understand?"

"Yes."

"Good."

"Above all, what you see and hear in this place stays here. Here. Do you understand?" She turned to me and looked at me with desperation, as if she might strangle me like the chickens she had been butchering if I didn't comply. Loyalty to her mistress was paramount, I gathered. "It is not only the writing that is to be kept secret, but also the queen's personal life. You'll have Obed to answer to, not me, if you transgress." Without waiting for me to answer she turned and kept marching.

"Of course," I offered, working to keep up.

We were moving past courtyards open to the sky that had been floored in brilliant colored and gilded mosaics but were now broken and smashed. A few chipped, stuccoed gold leaf columns still rose gracefully to the ceilings, and there was a splashing pool now stagnant, which must have held fresh water in the days before destruction. An old terraced garden, now choked with vines, tumbled into view as some of what must have been the queen's retainers busied themselves, cascading from one room to the next. An unfilled but magnificent and vast pool with an island designed to float in its middle caught my eye as we continued our whirlwind tour. My mind spun to a past of former decadence that I could not digest. One room I glimpsed had walls the color of the seas and sky, and as I passed I could see that it was oddly filled with life amidst all the destruction: filigreed bird cages studded with gem-like exotic trilling songbirds. I curled my fingers into my palms, knowing I should not ask, but I yearned to touch just one. Delicate twitters of varying complexity lifted to the sky, then drifted up and out, freed on the summer breeze to freshen the dry wilderness beyond as Joanna and I continued moving.

Soon we began winding up the shallow steps of a wide pitted marble staircase and I ran my hand on the cool banister. In one room of the turret to which we ascended we passed sheets of cream silk billowing on the breeze as men-servants changed bed linens in a room otherwise empty of any furniture. Each room was vast, a crumbled empire unto itself. We whisked past an expansive view out over the Dead Sea fifteen miles in the distance, its haze shrouding the town below. I could understand why the queen would feel no need to leave when she was here; here she would have all a person could desire even amidst the ruin—every luxury, every sensory experience—all except the real world.

Joanna and I slowed, arriving at a small room covered with an ornate brocade fabric. She brought me in and sat me down on a plain stone bench that wobbled as I shifted my weight. I pulled my skirts about me, and she began examining me—turning my hands over to make sure my nails were clean, removing my head covering and checking my hair to make sure I had no lice. She looked in my ears, then tapped me on the chin, telling me to open my mouth. She ran a finger under my lips around my gums, and when I tried to withdraw she cuffed my head.

"Submit. I have to know you are clean enough to be in the queen's presence; it is my job to keep her healthy and safe from pestilence. During these several months you will be here you may come when you are in your cycle, but you must let me know. You must have adequate coverage; if you do not, simply let me know and we will supply you with rags."

"We're not that poor!" I objected.

Unfazed, she continued, "The queen must never smell you. If you need a bath, ritual or otherwise, you may arrange with me to have one at the end of the day before you go home. We have *mikva'ot* here. Keep your gums clean and your breath fresh; we also have plenty of rosemary and cinnamon to chew on. Our standards of cleanliness don't just have to do with the laws of purity. The royals are more used to cleanliness, more like the Greeks. You must not offend in any way."

I nodded, large-eyed. From our hovel to such opulence! I tried to imagine what it must have been like to have grown up like Joachim and Meira, cloistered from the dregs and cares of the dirty world outside, clean and pristine as it was humanly possible to be in a luxurious, sanitized, art-filled world of immaculate bodies and fresh clothing and proper manners. I merely looked down at my feet in their plain felt footwear.

True, the rules of the Law applied here, too, because the queen was a Jew; yet the Law was at an oblique angle to existence here, it seemed to me, whereas in my world it served as the sustaining structure, the sturdy framework to which we all turned our faces and hearts in spite of our material existence, miserable as it was. Here it was as if the smashed marble and stone, along with the proprieties, luxuries, and hierarchies of such a place, were the structure to which all had turned, the organizing principle, a law unto itself, created outside ordinary existence. Each sensuous room had been at its zenith a moral compass unto itself; now the entire construct was ruined.

Sated with sensation, I could only wonder if the queen had been so caged her entire life in each palace and fortress to which she had traveled. I wondered how such captivity would have affected a person's heart and mind. But these questions I could not ask, I was told. I could only draw my own picture from what I would observe, what I could glean from Nathaniel's stories on a few return trips to Jerusalem I made during my employ, and from anyone here who came into contact with the queen on a daily basis.

And so indeed, after I had been coming to the queen daily for about three weeks, I did make a brief trip back to Jerusalem for supplies and a visit to my aunt; I felt I could speak more forthrightly with Nathaniel, after my experiences coming to the old fortress, and I felt bold enough to pry him open with my questions. His story did much to satisfy my curiosity, yet left me with lingering questions.

"Imagine," he said one late afternoon when he had had a rare day off and I had come back through the winding streets of the gold-glowing city to find him in the hot dusk, eating a Persian watermelon on the rooftop of his small stone house.

"Imagine that you were once the beauty of the tetrarch's court, and you could command the attention of men from the highest positions across the Judean desert. And yet . . . your mother ruled you. Not the tetrarch, Herod, but your own mother." Nathaniel slurped the juice out of the rind and threw it to a passing dog that sniffed at it but then trotted off in disdain.

"What are you saying?"

"I never knew the woman—Herodias. But they say she had hooks deeper into her daughter than a carrion bird in a freshly hung carcass. They say it was really Salomé who lost her head, not the John they called the Baptist."

I had turned down my head and felt the saliva rise sour in my mouth. Perhaps I was better left to draw my own conclusions from being in the queen's presence, I had decided as I returned to my work at Machaerus. After all, I had no information yet with which to counter the picture Nathaniel painted for me.

So I had returned to Machaerus still inquisitive. Time would surely unfold some of what seemed so mysterious to me. In the meantime, at least I had a somewhat better picture of the situation than I did on that first day of work.

On this first day I felt it was all I could do to not stumble over my feet and blurt out unseemly questions. Indeed, I believed in all earnestness that I could get more input from the people around the queen as I worked and ate and lived in the desert wilderness town, and so I intended. For the moment, Joanna raised me up by my hand, and it was evident all talking was to cease.

As we came out into the corridor again, a warm breeze from somewhere outside wafted up and bathed my face. Joanna tucked her chin into her chest as we drew up in front of the curtain through which I would enter daily for the next several months as I recorded the queen's words. I prayed silently to Adonai that I be pleasing and that I do my work well. Joanna watched my face as I stepped through the opening, her own face now composed.

Red silk banners streamed from the ceiling, dancing in the hot wind spilling in from the sea and the mountains below expansive windows. Sparing no luxury, servants had transported lush green palms that hid the crumbling gold leaf, and succulents masked wreckage in every corner. While plainer now than it had been once, the room retained its structure, eschewing straight lines; each transition from material to material was curved, inconclusive, flowing into the next. A small furry animal slept, sunken, beneath piles of embroidered pillows sewn in every hue of magenta, pink, red, and orange on a bed surrounded by delicately carved ivory pillars.

A woman in dark gray robes, in the dress of a widow and looking, to my Jerusalem-educated eyes, to be Greek, and wealthy, stood with a stack of parchment in her hands. From behind me Joanna looked at her, then said, "Thank you for coming, Miriamne. My mistress is tired."

"Theophile. My name is Theophile," but the woman's voice faded at the end, as if she were trying to impress upon her audience an unimportant fact. Then she raised her face to Joanna and glanced back at the queen.

"I will see that when the document is finished it gets passed on to the appropriate people who can deliver it to the bookmaker." With those few words, she gathered her cloak about her and left. She threw a look over her shoulder at me, and I felt a sad sinking wind go with her as she brushed past me and exited.

I froze. Joanna picked up my hand and touched it to the mezuzah, then to my lips, and then kicked at my feet. I felt the cool limestone beneath my toes through the felt on my feet. Joanna pressed on my backside to shove me forward a little, and I stumbled a few steps into the room. I stood, feeling naked, before the lone woman in the room.

Across the room crouched the queen, whose loose gray hair fell about her shoulders and down her back. As she rose, swaths of indigo and purple silk striped with white bands cascaded about her. She raised her neck to the sky outside the window, her eyes closed, and ran her hands up the winding river of her body with a look on her face as if she were recalling old memories. Then, twisting her arms about her head with her hands pushing away as if she would shift from her the accompanying body memories, she began to spiral around, dancing. Toes banded in silver and gold teased from under her gown as she arched and folded, smoothly at first. Hair hid her face. Finally she slowed, arthritic, and as her hair collapsed to one side I could see pain in her face and tears wetting her cheeks.

She looked up and saw me, and I was frightened. My mother had told me of demoniacs who lived outside the town at the edges of the sea, in the Judean desert and the Moab mountains, in tight caverned hillsides. Were they any less bound than this woman before me? Was this a queen? Was I to take dictation from such a person? Nathaniel had said nothing of the rightness of her mind. I had heard of it only from Meira, a child.

Yet, in a simplicity of knowing then that I could not have described years later, in the dark pools of her eyes and seams of her once fresh face, I gained a channel to her past. As if my dream life somehow connected me to her life story, as if the wisdom of my people and centuries of our narratives handed down orally could construct her legend for me, through the eloquence of her mute movement, I began to dream a kaleidoscope of her life more vivid than any dream I had yet had in my young life.

2

Thirty-eight years earlier, the outskirts of Machaerus, in the desert

THE SMALL spring fed a tiny cluster of sun-bright yellow flowers couched in a verdant patch. Against the undulating vastness of the Judean desert and Moab mountains the lush riot of color resisted upward, a diminutive army of life against a gulping dryness. A hot sky push-pulled, pressing down as if to hold in place the struggling life, all the while offering up the flowers to the sun in a rite of spring sacrifice. A small bubble of water, issuing from a riverbed with rock walls flanking it, ran in rivulets in the direction of the larger spring from the Wadi Edom that supplied Machaerus. Soon each trickle of water submerged, disappearing into crevices, cutting under the soft red Nubian sandstone that underlay the town and its outskirts.

With her finger Salomé drew in the sand around the water, writing her name with long tendrils, sinuous: Salomé, then Sam, her mother's short name for her. A boy's name: yet she had never considered why her mother had nicknamed her a boy's name. Maybe she had wanted a boy instead of a girl, the thought occurred to her for the first time. Indeed, Herodias often introduced Salomé saying, "She's my boy." Salomé wanted to please her mother, but this was an instance that merely confused her; she couldn't figure out why Mumma did this. She hadn't said it for a while though, perhaps since Salomé had begun her flow, or maybe since she had begun dancing. Salomé drew a line from the spring, channeling its water to the written name so that it erased the etched Sam, leaving only Salomé. Sighing, with one sweep of her hand she wiped out an entire patch of the sand, bringing her hand up to shade her eyes and look through the channel of the rock walls toward the small city, taking in the stone buildings, which were hardly different in color from the earth around her.

She stood, adjusted her silk robes about her, and draped across her arm the dull flax outer tunic with which she would cover herself going into and out of the citadel. It had not been so easy to evade her servants for her walk up into the ravine, but whenever she could she found her way to this peaceful hiding place where no one could hustle and buzz about her. The impenetrable, abiding silence of the desert soothed her from the jangling din of the constant activity in Herod's palace. The only aspect of the palace that pleased her and helped her feel free within its walls was its bird's-eye view of the Dead Sea and surrounding wilderness and desert mountains. Some days as she stared out onto the vast hills around her, her mood seemed so volatile she didn't know who she was, and all she wanted was to be left alone, moving into the wasteland on which she looked, searching for solace in the deepening desert. Since she and Miriamne, her elder sister by two years, had returned from the Jordan River to seek out the charismatic man baptizing and forgiving people for their sins, Salomé had longed for the stillness of the desert, which seemed in its hush to envelope her and hold her heart close as Mumma used to hold her.

Miriamne had wanted to go and look for the rising prophet-star who supposedly heralded the arrival of the Messiah, a man of whom she had become enamored though she had never seen him. Everybody was going to seek him out, as if to reenact the Exodus, it seemed. There had been a lot of prophets recently, but for some reason this one caught Miriamne's attention—probably because she and Salomé had overheard Herod talking about the man with Herodias more than once. Yet when the girls had gone to see him, the effect produced on Salomé had come at the conclusion of the trip, a still small voice having worked its way into her heart long after the two girls had slept for several nights under billowing tents brought with their chaperoned caravan. Camels fully laden had carried all of their food and hygiene needs, providing them with the luxury to which they were accustomed. In this the young women differed from so many others who had come from smaller surrounding towns and cities, including some crazies, all of whom had slept out under the stars on only their coats, all to be blessed by the gaunt intense man proclaiming Messiah's arrival. Salomé had seen the strange shading of her sister's eyes as those of the Baptizer seemed to latch onto hers—but then they seemed to Salomé to settle on anyone who could withstand his gaze for any length of time. Salomé got the impression that when Miriamne looked, she yearned toward a man who fit her young soul's uncertain needs for love, whereas when the man John looked at her sister, all he saw was somehow something larger or deeper than Miriamne could yet comprehend. Salomé feared her sister was asking of love more than she knew.

They had stayed for several days on that trip, a trip somewhat surprisingly agreed to by her mother, Herodias, and her stepfather, Herod. After the first few nights, Salomé had crept out of their tent in the deepening dusk to wander away from the river and the groups of people so that she could be on her own in the silence, which seemed to call to her of more than this John's message of God's forgiveness. Standing upon an empty patch of land by herself, both the dim lamps of the camp and a fire far enough away to give her privacy, Salomé felt the night wind lift curtains of sand to brush across her face. She raised her hand to her cheek and felt the young skin there, wondering if it would feel more like the sand when she had grown old. That the prophet held some sort of attractiveness, and especially for her sister, made sense to her—a magnet between a young heart, and a soul plunging into hearts without fear. But as she cast her mind into the future, wondering with whom she herself would unite in marriage, she could only intuit a man clasping her to his body. Standing on tiptoe at the sensation, she crossed her arms over her chest in a hug and turned her face to the sky. Love. Rather, marriage. As royals, she and her sister were limited in their selection—but she didn't want to think about the choices that would be made for her in this regard. Frowning, she realized Miriamne ought to pay some attention to their reality.

Yet once the trip was over and they had returned to Machaerus, Miriamne and she having been baptized, Miriamne had seemed to shrink into a shell, pining for the man, as if he had drawn life from her and she could barely breathe without him. She had even stopped eating for a few days, and Salomé had worried for her. It was as if the only sustenance she wanted was words from him. But Salomé didn't understand, because John's words to all of them gathered at the Jordan, as they listened to him make proclamations of the prophet Isaiah long before him, had been harsh: he had called them "children of snakes," accusing them of leaning on their good name as children of Abraham in the face of God's wrath, threatening them with being thrown onto burning refuse heaps if they did not turn back to God. The royals who had come to the river were too elegantly clothed, John had berated them, and he had told them they should shed their outer garments and give them to those in need. What he said made sense—if one were poorly off; but Salomé and Miriamne were not. John was just shy of shaming them all in public, a behavior that Jews considered equal to death, but Salomé supposed he said these drastic things to exhort them to turn to God, just as his predecessors had done in the ancient days.

Well, seeing the prophet had been novel, anyway. But Salomé had not lost her head over him the way Miriamne had. At times in his lectures he was so vehement that Salomé saw spittle at the corner of his mouth, and she would look over to see how Miriamne reacted to that, but her sister seemed oblivious. It was as if her eyes saw only passion.

Finishing her musings about the recent trip, Salomé turned her face to the sun, then picked up her sandals and began feeling her way down the rock and sand bed, her toes gripping every undulation of the rock. Moving slowly she let the heat from the rocks penetrate her feet. As the surface became too hot, some of the rock having baked in the sun for the entire morning, she sought the shade of the rock wall on her right. A lizard slinked away. Salomé placed her hands on the cooler, shaded sandstone, but as she came to the end of the abutment and rounded the corner she jumped as she collided with a man coming down from the other side of the rock wall. She bleated a small surprised cry; he teetered, then went down on all fours to prevent his fall.

Covering her mouth, Salomé immediately saw that he was a common man, youthful, but weary and gaunt. She wondered if he was one of those crazy Essenes who went into the wilderness to pray—then remembered that most of them were on the other side of the Dead Sea, in their community. He gasped for air and looked at her from a depth she had never seen. Hanging off his shoulders was a common linen robe, blue faded thread running through it, and from it Salomé could discern that he was a holy man. The lingering sweat-scent of his body on her clothing as he had collided with her stayed in her nostrils; she noticed even under his robes the length of his legs and his well-proportioned frame, the bronze of his wrists and hands. Oddly, his feet were bare, but she tried not to stare at them. For a timeless space they simply looked at one another.

Because she was a young woman, and, for all he knew, in her time of impurity, she bowed her head and took a few steps back. Simply by touching him she had made him impure; he would now have to go to the ritual baths to cleanse himself. It was a grievous error, but how could she have known a man would be so near to her quiet, private place? How could she have imagined someone else out there in her wilderness? Surely there were better places for a man to pray clandestinely, if that was what he had been doing. Her thoughts betrayed an irritability born of her unrecognized attraction, even as she grew aware of a deliciously cinching feeling in the core of her body, below her belly. The sensation seemed to tighten lightly and spread a wave of pleasure down the insides of her legs; her face tensed, as if her body could be read on her face and he would know what she was feeling. She glanced down at her middle, confused, then quickly raised her head back up to look at him, but he wasn't looking at her—only toward the east. Like centuries of women before her, she smiled to cover any other emotion she thought he might detect, so as to seem only pleasing to him. Feeling foolish, as if she had swapped places with Miriamne in girlish adoration, she stood speechless and waited for his eyes to return to hers. Seemingly all reason had been wiped out of her mind, and she was at the mercy of her body's responses, waiting to see what would next surprise her about herself. Perhaps, the thought struggled to the surface to connect with the rest of her, perhaps this was what it meant to be enamored of a man.

Salomé had known only crushes on boys to this point in her life. Inside the palace walls, she had been able to play with any child she had chosen, and while she had had girl friends, she saw no difference between having boys as friends and girls as friends. Once, she had put up quite a fuss with Mumma when she wanted some of her friends to sleep out on a roof under the stars but Mumma had told her no boys. Two of the boys around her had taken her fancy, and one had even tried to kiss her, but he had been caught and whipped. At that point she had begun to pay more attention to why the protest was made about keeping boys from girls.

Why this attraction today expressed itself as irritation she couldn't have said, but the man did see it, and the bemusement on his lean face only aggravated her the more, as if she had been caught in a lascivious act. "Are you yet another temptation sent my way?" he murmured to her, noting her young attractiveness.

But then the laughter on his lips and the look in his eyes passed as if heaven and earth themselves had wiped clean his face, and he merely stood before her.

She bent her head slightly to him. "Forgive me my transgression," Salomé said, begrudging the apology.

"You didn't know what you were doing. You are forgiven," he said, looking directly back at her, an unfathomable sadness now playing across his face. "I wonder . . . do you know this feeling of forgiveness, and being forgiven?"

His eyes stayed on her face as he said this, but it was as if her heart sealed his words for later consideration, though now she had absolutely no idea why or what had happened. She sat down, puzzled by his directness. Why was he speaking of forgiveness? Who but God could forgive? She lowered herself to the ground and rocked back on her heels as he turned and walked away. He began to move off resignedly, as if the wilderness were indeed the sword of which Lamentations spoke, a sword on which he must impale himself. With his back toward the sea, heavy, he seemed to take up the sun-orb itself on his shoulders so as later in the evening to be responsible for setting it behind the hills. Such a heaviness she had not seen in a man, even in the one with whom Miriamne was now so in love. The girl watched him and wondered who he was that he would speak to her with such boldness. Only her mother spoke to her so directly. But whereas her mother's command was frightening, his was . . . compelling. Her young mind boggled at these thoughts flowing through her. She sat transfixed.

After a few minutes of watching the man recede into the distance, she adjusted her robes and rose. This time in her walk she swayed her hips a bit, violating her mother's admonition to avoid doing so, glancing up every small while to look over her shoulder at the man moving away from her, half hoping he would turn around and take notice of her. Most girls were taught to accentuate their curves as they walked, tipping the pelvis in a sliding action designed to both draw the eye while jingling the bells worn at the hips. She was the daughter of Herodias, who had married Herod Antipas, the weaker son of the great King Herod, so she had been taught a more dignified carriage.

Only in her dancing lessons was she allowed to fully sway the curves that seemed to have bloomed recently in her like the fertile honeysuckle vines entwined about the palace walls, whose growth had annoyed her mother. Herodias could occasionally be seen hacking at the honeysuckle with an ornately carved sword, a soldier's piece, when the vines began to creep into the windows of her bedroom. Salomé's was a burgeoning femininity that somehow seemed to assault her mother's senses, as if her daughter had overtaken her mother's attractiveness and her mother could do nothing to stop the growth. Salomé puzzled over this creeping coldness she perceived, hardly knowing how she had offended her mother. But she knew something had changed, that their closeness had diminished. She tried to figure out what Mumma wanted; what Mumma wanted was all that mattered.

Walking in from the desert and looking at the fortress as she closed distance to it, she felt its imprint on her more than the hot sands stealing up under her feet. "I will smother anything that tries to move out from under me," its stalwart presence declared from the height of land. Yet the land that it pinned down was an old woman's parched skin and bones, no conquest at all, a land lacking beauty, dull to its inhabitants. Salomé walked up alongside the aqueduct carrying gathered rainwater into cisterns inside and around the palace. Long legs and strong hips strode her up the saddle of land on which the Herod before her stepfather had erected that which he intended to protect his lands against invasion from the east. Humming to herself, her mind playing over the holy man who had walked in the direction opposite her, she went into the palace through the delivery entrance, removed her tunic, and ducked into a doorway to avoid being seen by some servants heading to a nearby corridor; she wanted to savor as long as she could the privacy she'd had in the desert. Coming into the great gathering place that was the triclinium, with its porticoes open to the sky and intricate floor mosaic, she passed by the room of captive rare birds, the splashing pool, and past the steam baths her mother used. She stopped in here, looking for her mother. Not seeing her, she continued toward the stairs.

A cooling breeze blew down from above. Salomé looked up, stopped, and stood frozen when she saw Herodias standing tall with a carrion bird on her arm. Salomé recognized it as a Shikra hawk, a small eastern variety, recently added to the palace collection. A dusty grey-brown coat with barring on its chest distinguished it. Its beak was sharp, designed for plucking and ripping. The bird's talons had been clipped and were encased in miniature leather boots that had been specially made; its beak was lashed shut with a fine twine. Looking down at Salomé, Herodias unwrapped the rope-muzzle with talon-like fingers, and the hawk opened its gullet in a wide, silent scream. Then it turned its dark beaded eyes on Salomé. In her other arm, Herodias held a string of mice, clotted blood in their matted fur. The Shikra hopped on Herodias's arm and jabbed at the carnage, wanting it.

"Where have you been?" Herodias turned accusatory eyes to her daughter. Herodias was strong-boned, regal, and held the bird in her grip such that Salomé saw the sinews on her forearms showing above her gold bangles. Her hands were meticulously manicured, belying the strength of her grasp. As she turned her forearm and manipulated the hawk into a position more comfortable for her, the bird flapped its wings. Today Herodias wore a simple silver and sapphire ornamentation on her head, and Salomé was taken with her mother's choice of a deep blue gown with gold threads running throughout. Her mother's figure, while imposing, had begun its creep downwards; her breasts were still full but not quite as eye-drawing as they had been, and there were days when she complained to her daughter about how her breasts ached for no apparent reason. Around her deep set

eyes there appeared the beginnings of crow's feet, though it must
have been sunlight from which they formed because she seldom
smiled at her daughter, or anyone, except when in a formal situation around her husband. Her hair was coiffed high in the intricate fashion of the day, and henna hid the gray that had begun its
inexorable spread. A few streaks of complementary blue powder
had been added to her hair as a highlight.

Looking at her, Salomé again wondered if the growing rift
between her mother and herself was due in part to her mother's
keen awareness of her daughter's beauty increasing even as her
own more rapidly seemed to wane, an awareness that had seemed
to sharpen her mother's observations and her tongue alike.

"I haven't been anywhere special Mumma, just, uh, I . . ."
Salomé stammered, about to begin a lie, but bewildered as to
why she would do so. She had always told Mumma the truth.
Yet more and more lately she was experiencing confusion in her
mother's presence, and while she couldn't have pinpointed her
response as bewilderment, she felt unsettled and knew something was different.

Herodias swung the mice string out toward the hawk and
it lunged at the offering, spiking two mice at once with its beak.
It gulped, twisting its head in a grotesque movement that Salomé
watched, entranced against her will. Herodias's eyes sparkled at
the gore, then caught the distaste on her daughter's face.

"What—are you squeamish, Salomé? Really, you must become inured to such bloodshed. It won't be the last that you will
see in your life. Butchery is the price that we pay to maintain our
positions. It's time you put aside your childish naïveté."

Salomé nodded up at her mother, but then averted her eyes
again, her stomach in turmoil. Thoughts again flew from her, as
they had when she had been in the presence of the man in the
desert—but the setting was far less pleasant this time.

Miriamne came running into the great room just then, laughing and being chased by two young men in a crack-the-whip. The

boys were cream-skinned and tanned from the sun, their frames still spare with their youth, the laughter in their eyes a glittering gift. Miriamne's dark curls bounced and the silken yellow scarf around her neck flew out behind her as the three of them splashed into the fountain in the center of the room, tumbling about one another like a litter of puppies. Sensing Herodias on high, they all straightened and gawked as they turned to see the spectacle of the bird outlined against the golden light filtering into the room. Laughter died on their faces when they saw Salomé and Herodias standing and facing each other, as if the two might rise up in battle at any moment. The young men stood riveted, fascinated with the bird and its prey, losing interest in their own catch. Miriamne moved backwards, the hem of her dress dripping from the fountain, and she bumped into some succulent plants. Her eyes began their habitual watering.

It was obvious that Miriamne, while she was Salomé's elder and would be married off first, was far less beautiful than her younger sister, and ungainly. Since she was ten she had been plagued with watery eyes. At first Salomé had thought it funny, but now she knew that it shamed her sister. Miriamne blinked, looking from the boys to the bird then to Salomé. Salomé was glad for her to have the boys running after her so. Still, it often riled Salomé that Miriamne was eldest and trying always to draw Mumma's attention. But Mumma's focus had always been on Salomé, and Salomé expected nothing less. At times, on Salomé's moody days, it seemed to her as if her mother had practically consumed her from the time she was an infant, planning Salomé as the ascendant child over Miriamne. Salomé had been old enough to remember that she had been nursed until she was five years old, but it was as if Herodias had somehow been sucking the life out of Salomé, rather than Salomé nourishment from her mother. Miriamne, on the other hand, according to the clucking of the wet nurses, had been handed off and weaned in the usual length of time. There was even speculation that Miriamne was not the daughter of Herodias's first union with Philip, Herod's brother, but born of one of several rumored illicit unions Herodias had made.

The younger sister had watched the elder's desperate rebellions to recapture her mother's eye and love; the small protests had become all too obvious in recent years, but each effort fell flat as her mother seemed merely bored with her oldest daughter. Now it seemed as if Salomé were suffering the same disenfranchisement. Miriamne, Salomé could understand, had looked elsewhere for love, attaching herself to almost anyone who came within her purview: music teachers, scribes, servants, and especially Salomé. Only slowly was Salomé becoming aware of Miriamne's great need for someone whose hair she could pet and wind her fingers in as Salomé had always done with Mumma, someone to whom she could chatter happily as they lay side by side on the cool silk bedspread in the dusk in a room overlooking the city.

Salomé's closeness with Mumma was simply the reality in which she had always lived; she had never meant to exclude her sister. But on her murkiest days of feeling unloved Miriamne would completely lose her temper, jolting Salomé into her sister's reality. Once, Salomé had walked in on Miriamne in her messed-up bedroom when she was in a fit of rage, throwing pillows about and exclaiming to one of the morning servants about an angry, violent dream that she said had made her wonder if perhaps she was really Herod's daughter rather than Philip's.

In a dawning recognition of her rivalry with her sister Salomé began to observe their interactions more acutely, having learned the skill intuitively from her mother, she supposed. Perhaps it was something that came easier with her growing up, as well. It was as if she could begin to actually think about such things. The girls' mutual interests notwithstanding, with time Salomé had grown more aware, and wary, of the contention between her sister and herself. Yet it was the last thing she wanted, as Mumma appeared to be drawing away as well.

"Girls, I want you to observe." From a pouch strung around her middle Herodias now pulled out by the head a small live bird of brilliant plumage, green-coated with a long slender bill and a red cap. Seemingly drugged or frozen in fear it moved a leg slowly, which Herodias caught with her other hand and swung up to the Shikra. In one last wiggle at freedom it struggled, swinging back and forth toward its tail, before the larger bird nailed it and guzzled it down.

"Mumma!" Salomé cried. "That was the little Green Bee-Eater, my favorite!" Herodias ignored her daughter.

Miriamne stood speechless, wiping her eyes and face. At that moment Herod came into the room with his own internal fanfare.

A sturdy man, his veins standing out in his forearms, Herod planted himself and stood next to a tall marble pillar of the hardest *meleke* limestone imported from Jerusalem. The marble jutted upright in the center of the room and had been erected there no doubt for one of Herod's ongoing projects. He looked first at Miriamne wiping her eyes, then at his wife, who held the bloody-beaked hawk on her arm. In a breath Salomé expelled her exasperation at the interruption; she knew the tetrarch was used to being the center of attention and any interaction with him upset the balance already established in a room. She may have been supposed to be close to him, being his stepdaughter, but Salomé recoiled at his presence, as if he created an intangible repelling field around him. Or maybe it was more a net than a field, a net that seemed to simultaneously entrap people and keep them at bay as if he could tolerate only his own presence in his own bodily sphere. And so she had stayed away from him as much as she could. She had heard the talk that he was weaker than his father had been, his father who had built so many palaces and fortresses after the Hasmonean rulers preceding him.

This incriminating weakness she had witnessed as a petty cruelty toward his servants and animals. Fortunately, he seemed to take only a passing interest in the birds. Yet further, Salomé had heard her mother's endless complaints that he never seemed to have the courage to use his influence as a tool as had Herod the Great, whom she knew some now called Herod the Brutal.

As long as she could remember, Salomé had shrunk from her stepfather in his presence, until one day, out wandering in the desiccated hills, it occurred to her like a flash flood coming down the wadi that her body's natural and unexplained reaction to him meant that she despised rather than feared him. She had sat still, drawing circles in the dust, as the cognition ran over her and she twitched with the connections she was making. Under a silent sky, only the passing clouds studding the sky had seemed to validate the new knowledge resting in her breast. Most of her mind's growing recognition had come to her in quiet spaces and times like this.

As a ruler Herod was less respected than his father had been. When the opportunity to marry the power-consuming Herodias had arisen he had slunk in through the side door, thinking that allying with her would increase his influence; perhaps they were simply two of a kind. Salomé had loved her father and her grief at her parents' divorce had remained stuck in her throat for years, making silence in the wilderness her comforting companion.

"Did those boys make you cry?" Herod's voice battered in Miriamne's direction with the fluttering commotion going on about him. He seemed stupidly unaware that his other stepdaughter had had her weepy eyes for quite some time now. Before waiting for an answer, he scowled at the young men, who exited quickly down a corridor, then barked at his wife, "I've been looking for that bird!"

Herodias rotated her neck to turn a chilling eye to the man who was the center of power and who now stood below her. It had been long since he had come to her bed, she had complained to Salomé, and her influence lessened if she could not keep him in her clutch. Even so, her growing contempt for him was obvious, Salomé thought.

Momentarily, all of them were mute, Herodias, Salomé, Miriamne, and Herod, in a rare moment of family togetherness. Herod next inserted life by clearing his throat.

"Tomorrow night, as you know, I celebrate my birthday! I have dignitaries from Galilee and this miserable quarter of Perea coming, and I need some entertainment for my guests. I want that bird—I want to show off its skill. Young Obed's idea was to release some mice out of a bag and let the bird fly about the room to capture them. But I think it will make the women scream if they see mice running up under their skirts," he guffawed, "so we are having to come up with a variation. I'll surprise you, and it will be sure to astonish." He pressed the information in the direction of his wife, then pulled back to turn to Salomé.

"I need one other thing." He looked back up over his shoulder at his wife, the limestone pillar standing near him and his stepdaughter. "I need some dancing. You've been practicing, I'm told." His back to Herodias, looking at Salomé, he reached a stout finger to her white neck and ran it up toward her ear, moving aside a tendril of her hair. She turned her head slightly, tensing her jaw, and felt the muscle on the side of her neck stand out. Herod continued tracing her form, not facing his wife, and in a deft move intended to avoid his wife's watchful eye he moved his hand down Salomé's front to quickly pinch her nipple. Her hand flew up to cover herself, and she looked up, young rage boiling on her face as she looked helplessly at her mother. But her mother had become strangely interested in the bird's wings, and seemed oblivious. Salomé turned her eyes back to the odious man before her and shrank away. For a moment he peered past her shoulder, frowning at Miriamne, his disappointment with her showing plainly on his face. Whether it was that she had not been born a male, or that she was too unadorned and would not do for his purposes Salomé didn't know, but she was so filled with rage and shame that she could hardly breathe. At least, thank heavens, he left Miriamne alone. She would keep Herod from Miriamne even if she could not keep him from herself.

Narrowing her eyes at him, barely veiling her contempt, she strategically redirected her stepfather's attention: "Would you like to see me dance before the dinner, your Highness?" Salomé bowed her head slightly, and took a step back from being within his reach. But she was torn: at the same time that she saw herself protecting her sister, she was concerned that she might trump Miriamne with her offer of dancing. With her offer Salomé reached dimly for a chance to push back at her mother's negligence, trying to take charge of the situation. While she had never reconciled herself to calling Herod father, and while she recognized he was an attractive man of a certain sort, she none-theless detested his brutishness and his loud presentation. Why her mother fancied him she didn't comprehend. She never saw them touching. But like the tug in her lower belly when she had seen the holy man in the wilderness, she now felt a string pull-ing her in opposition to her mother, as if something moved her, puppet-like, despite herself. Her face flinched a little as she made the offer, but she looked steadfastly at her stepfather, even as she avoided her mother's now rock-hard face.

"Yes, perhaps. Well, maybe. No. Surprise me. You are so luscious"—here he almost lunged at her—"I trust you can im-press me—as well as some men who may have offers for you. And I have some new musicians and instruments in for the mu-sic we will have." Seeking approval for this information, he leered up at Herodias, who only glared at him.

Salomé stared at the splashing pool, sinking into a reverie. It was a childish practice she used frequently, this prodding of a pleasant memory to distract her from the exhausting and never-ending whip of her mother's need to be the most recognized in the room. As a shaft of sunlight illuminated her mother for a moment, Salomé receded to some old memories of time spent with her mother, memories that painted a golden aura-filled past and gave the girl a sense of immutable sanctuary. She remembered nestling with her mother on a chilly morning deep in some furs on a luxuriant bed. Sleepy, they had both drifted, spooning, and the sun had come out through the piling clouds framed by the large stone window. She had felt her mother's breathing, the rise and fall of her chest as her own breath rhythm fell in with Herodias's. When she awoke, Herodias had ordered some warm goat milk for Salomé and held it for her as she drank from the shallow clay bowl. This warm scent of security stayed with Salomé through her years of growing up, servants and nurses coming and going, despite all the traveling in caravans from fortress to fortress. It was the feeling to which she returned to comfort herself late at night while her mother had slowly withdrawn as Salomé slid toward womanhood.

It seemed they had been happier before with Philip, before this strange swine of a man had come into their lives. But there the new father was, before her now, and as she came out of her dream state she felt he was asking of her something of which she barely knew the power. Yet with the eyes of an infant beginning to focus she sensed that she held a rising influence over him, a sway her mother could no longer match. She decided she would use her new power, regardless of its effect on her mother or her sister.

Salomé turned to face Herod more fully just as the bird rose tall on Herodias's arm. Expanding its feathers in a display of intimidation, it let out a piercing screech that finished in a guttural strangle. Salomé, both at the shrill assault and in a deep instinctual fear that her mother could read her guilty shaming mind, ran to clasp Miriamne's hand and pull her out of the room, leaving Herod and Herodias standing face to face.

3

The next day

Salomé awoke early on the dawn the next day, savoring the realization that she had dance practice for the upcoming dinner.

Birds chittered in the vines, flushing out the last of dead winter growth into the coming spring. A curling air from the Dead Sea sent up a salt finger stretching toward Machaerus, steeping small desert flowers and lifting their fragrance to infuse the wilderness outside the town. Lower down on the north slope, near the town's stone houses and the cisterns dotting the waterless hillside, olive trees rustled, as if their dry lace above the ground and below it created a seine holding in place the blues and tans of the sky and earth.

Salomé held out a long slender arm and contemplated her trimmed and buffed nails. Her thoughts wandered to her sister. Once out of the triclinium, Miriamne's fingers had slid from Salomé's. Salomé had fallen back behind her sister, whose head was down while she wiped a tear now and then and they both walked, presumably forgotten by their elders, to their rooms. Having arrived at Miriamne's room, with one long look back up at Salomé, who read the look as pregnant to bursting with heart secrets she would like to share but dared not, Miriamne pushed aside the curtain and disappeared behind it. For her part, back in her own room Salomé had sent away her maid servant, then brushed out her silken hair down to her waist with the sow's bristle brush, and bound it up to create curl in it for the next day.

Salomé still liked to pet her mother's hair in her mind's eye as she had when she was a child when they would get dressed together in the mornings. Her thoughts shuttled back to Miriamne, who had lately admitted almost no one but her sister into her room. Salomé couldn't remember the last time Mumma had been in Miriamne's room, though she was frequently in Salomé's, so being the one with the most access to Miriamne Salomé wondered about the peculiar look she had seen on her sister's face. She ran through several scenarios in her mind—Miriamne accusing her of being Mumma's favorite, of playing both sides—her mother against her sister—and in this image of betrayal Miriamne wept in earnest, while Salomé defended herself. Unspooling the fantasy further, Salomé sensed for the first time the abandonment and tension her sister felt, knowing Miriamne had neither her stepfather's nor her mother's love first. In this manner, as if Salomé ruled the beating hearts of twins connected, she created in her mind her sister's reality, as she often did for other people as well. At times it seemed anyone observing could have noticed that Miriamne engaged with Salomé in a constantly alternating game of closeness, then fury, as she vied, too late, for her mother's affections. Yet others' opinions notwithstanding, as if shaping her own rare bird from her thoughts alone, Salomé placed herself in blameless relation to her dejected sister and fashioned Miriamne's world—a world that might have been accurately imagined, or not. It was the only way Salomé felt any authority over this caged, minutely observed existence of hers, this structure produced by her mother's illicit union—the bond forged of her stepfather's power and her mother's control. Salomé's mental manipulation, along with periodic escaping to the desert, provided her a sense of relief and freedom she could attain neither in the palace nor under her mother's vigilant eye.

Miriamne appeared to be escaping in another way. For a few months now she had been playing games with the food on her plate, as if in so doing she could gain some advantage over her mother who, try as she might, could not make her daughter eat. Miriamne would either take her food by herself in her room, feigning (so Salomé believed) illness, or she would take smaller portions and simply push around on her plate the hummus, pita bread, cheese, and delicacies the palace cooks prepared for the family nightly. No amount of her mother's stiff-jawed response, threatening, even yelling, was having any effect. When Salomé had questioned her sister about it, she would laugh it off, then distract Salomé with gossip about the most notorious rich Greek wives or by showing her the latest silks and jewels brought on caravans from lands to the east. Salomé had been agreeable, loving to touch the fine cloths, but she had snuck glances at her sister's shrinking breasts, and in the bath she could see her sister's hip bones showing now. Miriamne had become secretive lately, so just as Salomé felt her mother pulling away, hugging and touching her less, she also felt Miriamne moving off to a place to which she was having a hard time gaining admittance. She resolved to coax out of Miriamne this morning what ailed her. A certain amount of detachment from the sisterly contest she could tolerate, but not this much. And there was a secret Miriamne appeared to keep that Salomé's imagination had not even begun to weave into existence for her sister.

Salomé slid off the sheets and covered herself with a pale yellow silk robe, then moved to the broad window with its view on a sunken garden of miniature date palms. The distant olive trees had stilled their rustle and the sky had sprung up out of their lace net, flinging birds into the thin dry air. Salomé watched two in particular wing to the north, up toward the Galil, where peasants lived. Pondering, she turned back into the room and sat on a cushioned chair of ivory, running her fingers one over the other. When this began to bore her, she jumped up and walked on tip-toe to the hanging dance costume that she would wear for Herod's party. Her hands tinkled the silver and gold bells, bangles, and tiny mirror pieces sewn to green and blue gossamer-thin silk. She knew that she could make the gown and its veils alluring, dimly aware of the new-found power of her beauty; Miriamne's jealousy was the greatest validation of that realization, but she also felt a calling in the slicing rotation of her hips she had recently mastered in dance practice. Miriamne would watch and resent, and heaven only knew how her mother would react when she danced tonight. A small smile curled the corner of her mouth as she twirled a little, arching her brows, puckering her lips in mock invitation to kiss, her hands twisting above her head in spirals as she imagined the sounds of the cymbals and flutes and drums. Her thighs warmed, and she placed a hand on her belly, pressing her pelvis into a soft circular motion. While she was not fully conscious of why she wanted to dance for Herod, given her distaste for him, she allowed herself to believe that she was only doing as bidden by the tetrarch. She could not yet express that dance freed her, gave her room to move out from under her mother's eye, away from the strictures of her upbringing, into her own free flight.

Then without any warning the curtain was flung aside as Herodias burst in with Miriamne on an invisible string behind her. Caught, embarrassed, Salomé stopped dancing abruptly as Herodias stood before her, one eyebrow arched while the rest of her face remained flat and impenetrable. Miriamne's head popped out from behind her mother. She struggled to control a giggle.

"Sam! Do you know what time it is?" Herodias demanded.

"Yes, Mumma, I know what time it is." Salomé kept her voice flat as her mother's face, though the nickname rankled.

It occurred to Salomé that her mother might have asked permission to enter, but the anger she could have felt she buried deep within, as if there were not enough space in her bedroom for both the feeling and her mother; somehow her mother crowded out all emotion, when she wasn't trying to appropriate it. Realizing such thought was dangerous, because any feeling she showed on her face would surely leave her exposed to her mother's acute observation, Salomé's face clamped resolutely shut. She stood placid, hands at her side now, and focused on the crease in her mother's left earlobe. Quiet ruled the room. The blue and green sparkle dress fluttered behind Salomé in a breeze that blew in from the courtyard below, as if Salomé's spirit had flown from her body to quicken the costume, escaping the claims of Mumma.

Imperiously her mother stated, "Today I have something planned for you and your sister." She turned on her heel to look back at Miriamne. "I want you to go to that imprisoned prophet, John, and make a visit to him asking him his . . . forgiveness. That's what he's been doing for people, I understand. I don't see why we shouldn't benefit. Perhaps you will also garner information about the prophet Yeshua. Since all the men your stepfather has sent have been unable to obtain anything more than gibberish from John, I have decided a woman should go. He will be more receptive to you because you are women. And I believe he has displayed a certain . . . concern . . . for your sister. I can't go because I would not be able to look at him without spitting." Here she craned her head on her long smooth neck to glance out the window. "So I have decided you and your sister will go. Miriamne is . . . willing," and here she rotated to look over her other shoulder at Miriamne again, whose face appeared to melt into the pools created by her welling eyes. "You." She pointed a long finger at Salomé. "Go with her. Herod has placed him in a cistern below the walls here; Miriamne knows which one. Tell the guards you have my permission."

She turned her hooded eyes to look at her eldest daughter. "You have an opportunity here, for us, not just yourself. Your stepfather has forbidden anyone to speak with John. I give you permission. I know you will perform perfectly, as the eldest should do. What you discern may be of great consequence for us all. At least try to make me proud. Salomé, if she fails in any way, pick her up—cover her blunder."

Salomé stood a little straighter, like a feral animal rising on two legs to challenge her mother's directive, resisting intuitively and inexplicably. Consciousness of her reaction again bloomed in her mind. Then as if tired by the very thought of effort at confronting the creature before her, Salomé's shoulders rounded and she changed her focus to her sister. Her thin, weepy sister, tightly kinked hair, odd-jawed, gentle in a way Salomé was not, wound a string from her dress around her fingers and looked up at her mother.

Salomé stared at Miriamne, perplexed at the complication into which her mother was inserting herself. John was one of many prophets who had risen in this time of wretched unrest slicing through Judea, but he had distinguished himself by baptizing people in the Jordan River, praying as if he could give God's forgiveness for their sins. That boldness was attention-getting enough, but what had so unnerved Herod had been, first, John's declaration that the King of the Jews was coming soon, and that this one would topple Herod's reign. Herod had wanted the label King of the Jews for himself, but had only achieved being tetrarch, ruler of a quarter of the lands his father had divided up between the surviving sons he had not murdered. It was impossible for Salomé not to be aware of some of the political shiftings going on around her, given Herod's flamboyance about it all. John had done himself no favors when he had further angered the nervous and largely impotent would-be king by alienating himself from the very seat of power that could have protected and promoted his moral campaign: he denounced Herod's having married Herodias. Offensively, even. He had made no bones about what really was fact—that Herod had lusted after Herodias, his brother Philip's wife, and so she and he had arranged divorces from their spouses. That in and of itself was a pretty good trick, since Jewish women were not allowed to divorce their husbands; only husbands could do the divorcing, even for something as slight as burning dinner, it was said. While Herodias had never cooked a dinner in her life, she did stretch her behavior somewhat beyond poor cooking. Of course, everyone knew that Philip had been cuckolded long before he had been divorced; even Salomé could remember Herod's late night visits when she was very young. Herodias had never hid her contempt for Philip, flirting with the taut, muscular Herod from the time she had been betrothed to Philip. She had connived with Herod from the beginning, she had later confided to Salomé, ever intent on gaining the power she wanted, all the while standing in Herod's shadow and behind her own hard, regal beauty. Her attention to Salomé during that time had been the only small softness she had allowed herself, and now even that she had closed off as Salomé's exquisiteness surpassed her mother's.

Rousing herself from her reverie, then staring at Miriamne, Salomé concentrated her efforts on wondering what role Miriamne was playing in this latest intrigue of her mother's. The sad silliness of it! Could the gaunt Miriamne have fallen in love with the wraith-like prophet who they said fed only on locusts pounded to powder and mixed with thin wild honey? Was this possibly the secret Miriamne had been keeping? Curiosity pulling Salomé forward on a filament, she looked back at her formidable mother and simply, sweetly answered, "Yes, Mumma, we'll go visit the prophet." No daydream to past coziness took her now; she felt her mother's impending snare and wanted to spring from it.

Before her daughter had even finished agreeing, there never having been any question that Salomé would respond as her mother wished, Herodias strode over to the diaphanous dance dress and fingered it, causing it to tinkle.

"It's not your color," she clipped. Dropping the fabric she turned and marched out of the room.

4

The same day

Salomé practically barged into Miriamne's room once she had put on her simple linen tunic for going to visit the prophet, wanting to avoid ostentation. Perhaps in hopes of being somewhat attractive while still plainly dressed, Miriamne had chosen a light blue variation of her sister's robe. They lit out, arm in arm, winding their way from the west wing to the east, cheeks close together, feeling supported in their joint effort though it had been commanded by their mother—perhaps even more secure in the adventure because of the directive.

As they passed the room of the rare caged birds Salomé glanced in and saw the hawk from the previous day clasped onto the back of a female hawk, its head back, throat to the sky, as the male dug its claws into the female's back in a mating embrace. Salomé pulled up short and at her hip came Miriamne. They stared for a moment in fascination at the act, then averted their eyes. Was all mating like this? Was it not caressing? Salomé put her head close to Miriamne's and as they continued on engaged her in talk of the latest eye powder women were applying to their eyelids. Pushing the repugnant image of the birds out of her mind she quickened her pace and clasped Miriamne's arm more tightly as if to protect her. In this close chattering way they proceeded outside the cooled building and into the day's heat. Down the aqueduct they hurried, looking off to the north and down upon the lower town as they descended, heading for some unused outlying cistern areas that had once supplied water in an elaborate system to the palace but had fallen into disuse when Herod had replaced them with a more sophisticated Roman water system.

The air was sweetly fragrant as they came into the town's market area. Passing by the crowded stalls displaying colored fabric from remote lands, they ooh'd and aah'd, letting their fingers run over the subtle hues and soft cloth. When they had been younger Herodias had taken them together on trips like this in the various cities they moved to and from, and had allowed them to touch all they could lay their eyes on, so that they had both developed quite a discriminating expertise about fabric and its origins and the fastness of the dye applied to it.

Once, Herodias had selected for Salomé a clothing trunk made of some sort of swarthy wood imported from the east. It was rubbed to a dark sheen, tooled with the tightest and finest swirling engraving she had ever seen, ornamented at its corners, inlaid with silver and garnets. Smaller than most of her trunks, still it was large enough to hold trinkets, a dress or two, and special mementos. Salomé had hopped in excitement, desiring it from the first, so Mumma had purchased it for her. Thereafter, only the finest and most unusual of her belongings were placed in the trunk. When Salomé had selected the dress in which she intended to dance for Herod, she had first run it past Miriamne for her approval, and Miriamne had declared it the most beautiful piece of sewing and embroidery she had ever seen; Salomé had stored it in what by now seemed to her the almost magical trunk. Salomé hoped likewise to help Miriamne select fabric when it came to helping her sister choose her wedding attire; she envisioned cloaking Miriamne in the traditional light muslin veil covering the face, helping her design her hair style, even participating in the bridal bathing process that the women did for one another. But this kind of idyllic closeness she developed with her sister had been beyond Mumma's watchful gaze, and it gave Salomé another path to that cozy feeling, the sense of security for which she had so much nostalgia, as if they were like any other comfortable Jewish family. As the sisters walked, Salomé looked eagerly into Miriamne's face to see there the excitement of her love for this prophet to whom they now went.

This flight of fancy in her mind lifted her to the stirring she had felt for the holy man in the desert the previous day, and Salomé listened with only half attention as Miriamne spilled over with her own delectable yearnings for a love of her own, adult, beyond both her sister and her mother.

Making eye contact occasionally with Miriamne, surrounded by the din of the market, but still weaving her internal world as they walked, Salomé soon arrived at the dismal memory that Herodias had stopped taking them on outings together. They had moved so many times, each time to a different fortification of Herod's as he tried to retain hold of his quarter, that a tiredness had set in. No longer did Herodias take an interest in the locals. Engaging less with the Greek and Roman worlds beyond the palace walls, they had all turned to more internal diversions. Salomé had begun excelling in her dance, past Miriamne's capabilities, who seemed to have clubs for feet. Salomé suspected Miriamne began to resent the grace with which her younger sister moved, and her absorption in it, as if it transported her away from the enmeshment of their contorted family. It also became obvious at that time that the girls' looks began to diverge, and Salomé noticed that when Miriamne realized she was not as attractive as her sister her tongue sharpened. This she must have picked up from Herodias. Salomé could not seem to breach the wilderness of their new estrangement, which was peculiarly simultaneous with that from her mother. So Salomé had taken to walking outside the town or city for solace, when she wasn't spinning and gyrating for her teachers, practicing the undulating dance that seemed to fling from her hips the disappointment and youthful sadness at the loss of her sister's affections and the snugness with her mother. Some days Salomé felt as though she spun from sister to mother, mother to sister, sometimes touching on Herod, not knowing which way to turn for love, confused as to whom to throw her affections, wanting only affection in return.

At first, when Salomé began her dancing lessons, Herodias seemed to see her youngest daughter's growing beauty and movement skills as a tool, so she took an interest in promoting her daughter's attractiveness, showing her off. Salomé had basked in Mumma's renewed favoritism as if it were a sound substitute for genuine concern and love, but there was a hollowness she began to sense.

Still, this was a relatively happy period for all of them, in which Herod and Herodias had seemed contentedly in love with one another. Salomé often saw them playful, exchanging affectionate touches even in front of the servants and guards. Herod treated his new possession like the royalty she so longed to be. He supplied for her the pomegranates she craved, and they would eat them side by side, slurping up the juice together, staining their fingers red. He obtained the rarest blue dye for her hair, making her the envy of all the Hellenized women, and from the east he bought for her a carved ivory bed frame that Salomé heard whisperings about by the servants, about the way her mother would grasp the headboard when Herodias and Herod made love. Apparently the servants had walked in on the lovers more than once.

But it was during that time that Herodias was swallowed by a narcissism that made her forever foreign to Salomé. The tetrarch and his wife had shared their love of rare birds and built a small aviary that Herodias took with her wherever they moved as Herod built his puny territory, trying to achieve on a small portion of lands the fame his father had achieved with so much more. Yet he was a client of Rome through and through, and Herodias began to evidence a growing disgust and then contempt for him at some of his decisions. In recalling this time, a tangent, the occurrence of which sort had begun to puzzle Salomé as she had grown older, interjected itself into her musings. She recalled the strange man in the wilderness she had met, his eyes, and she could not conceive of him ever feeling contempt for one he supposedly loved. Yet in thinking of Herod the feeling made sense to the girl, because he seemed to command no broad respect, and both Salomé and Herodias were aware of the servants' and townspeople's and guards' whispered mockery. Like a snake shedding its skin, the illicitly married couple's love had fallen off Herodias so that it was as if Herodias stood looking in a glass at only her naked self under a pale moon. Herod would still probably have clasped his wife to him fiercely, defending her and his fortress. He was proud of that beauty that she seemingly held on to with that grasp of her hand on the headboard, but there was no softness or compassion between them anymore, and his hold on her loosened; the grip fell, slack. Compassion was a sentiment that did not come naturally to either one of them, it seemed, and it was evident that they were each too fearful of losing their coveted power to dissolve into nostalgia for their early courtship.

So while Mumma had treated Salomé for a while as if she were the latest uncommon bird, the hardening of her mother's disappointed love for her husband could not but settle into Salomé's awareness. Sometimes Salomé felt as if she were to blame somehow, as if by growing more mature she had supplanted her mother in her stepfather's eyes. It was not a burden she could bear, even if she had wanted. So she flung the guilt from her as she danced, creating with the field of her hips an ever-expanding internal world as she circled and whirled, half waiting to see what she might catch in the ephemeral net she cast, half waiting to see what she could create or destroy with her hips.

The girls burst into the freeing sunlight of the settling afternoon. The valley of the eastern lands lay as far as they could see, heat waves rippling the landscape. Purple-shaded, the mountains of Moab hid a pale moon rising, spilling over early to slimly balance the opposite setting sun. Behind them, as they turned their heads for a full circle view, the haze of the Dead Sea bracketed them in from the west. They followed the long line of the stone aqueduct, the hot powdered ground dented by their footsteps, as they headed toward the cisterns. Salomé was unsettled, because if, out of desperation, Miriamne had fallen in love with a prophet under Herod's disfavor, she could see nothing good coming of it.

As they walked she felt pebbles rolling under her feet. Hearing a small din off to one side of the ravine, she and Miriamne turned their heads to see a rubbish heap down the slope. There were some men pushing about a pile of bones mixed in with piles of grayed and brittled refuse, all of which was burning. She grasped Miriamne's hand and pulled her forward, wanting desperately to keep their outing light and unpolluted by the sordid backdrop of reality. Gravity drew them down the saddle-slope the aqueduct traveled, and soon they were skipping. About three quarters of the way down Miriamne pulled her sister off onto a smaller side trail, and the walls of the ravine steepened around them. Like goats they gingerly picked their way around the side of the mountain, passing a few cisterns that were filled to varying degrees with water channeled from the aqueduct. Soon, out of the sun's fading light, they rounded a corner to arrive at their destination.

Deeply sunken, the waterless cistern was a dark toothless gaping mouth, open in a shriek. Miriamne and Salome hesitated in the face of its swallowing threat and looked upon the three guards standing around it who had been drawing lewd pictures in the sand. When they saw the girls approaching, they wiped out the figures and immediately stood erect. One of them, recognizing the girls, bowed.

"We are here on Herodias's order to visit with the prophet below," Salomé explained.

The guard, hoary-bearded and a father for many years, raised an eyebrow but again bowed. "Lady. The tetrarch has forbidden anyone to see the prophet."

"Yes I know that, but my mother has given permission. I suggest you not cross her."

"As you wish. Let us lower you down. The man poses no threat to you," he said in an undertone, glancing at the other two guards. He walked around the curve of the cistern and pulled up a rope ladder that had been anchored beneath a huge piece of basalt rock, then dropped it over the side, calling out to a shadow below who did not respond.

Miriamne's eyes had begun watering again; she ducked her head and wiped them on her cloak, signaling that Salomé should descend first. The guard held out a stubby, calloused hand, pursed his lips, and did his best to steady the young lady as she worked to keep her weight balanced on the ladder. He had heard the stories of her dancing, and though he had turned away his eyes, he had noticed the curve of her figure as her cloak had swung open. The ladder was easily strong enough for the two lightweight girls, so he gestured to Miriamne that she could begin her descent even as Salomé was still on her way down. She did, but Salomé glanced up as she felt the stretch and warp in the ladder above her. A movement of cool air from below wafted up, as if a sigh had escaped from the prophet below, but still no greeting rose. Not wanting to look down, Salomé kept her gaze at eye level and continued.

She breathed in the dank and cooling air of the cistern, looking at the stone before her face as she focused on each rung. One of the deeper wells, it sank about forty feet. She descended into growing twilight. Why this cistern had come into disuse she wasn't sure, but it was a perfect round prison, inescapable, unless one had the claws of a bird and the feet of a goat. Or a miracle of God. Suddenly she was grateful for her warm bed, soft linens, and bountiful food. Her foot touched dry dust. She let go of the last rung and turned around.

John sat before her, his arm draped loosely over one knee, his head turned only slightly in her direction. He splayed all five

fingers on the ground before him and rocked forward, pushing himself up off his hands with effort, looking almost like a
carcass.

They stood facing one another. He was tall, taller than she
had realized the first time they had gone to see him. His beard
had grown unchecked, and was knotted toward the end; she
could smell him, but it was a mild and not unpleasant odor, as
if the sweat had dried on him long ago. Bare to the waist, his
skin was nut-brown from the sun. Every rib showed, as did the
veins in his forearms. Of the same thinness as her sister, but at
least ten years her senior, Salomé now saw him as a beautiful
masculine specimen. He had a quality similar to the man she
had seen in the desert yesterday, but there was a discernible if
ineffable distinction. Thrusting a look into eyes garrisoned by
the heaviest and darkest eyelashes she had ever seen on a man,
Salomé had to withdraw her own gaze, not able to counter a
depth she could not fathom. She looked away and turned around
to see Miriamne finishing her descent. A thrill of fear crept up
her spine as she wondered what her sister had gotten herself into,
and how she, Salomé, could protect from their mother the in-
nocent love she suspected grew in her sister's heart because her
mother's avariciousness toward her daughters' emotions knew
no limits. If Salomé had been pressed at that moment, she would
not have believed she would have been up to the task. Perhaps
the prophet could provide some saving grace to shield them all.

Miriamne stood looking at the cistern wall in front of her,
between the ladder rungs, wiped her eyes once, then turned,
shoulders squared to her prophet. She looked straight at him,
and he turned his gaze to her. The stillness at the bottom of the
well engulfed the three of them; no one moved. Then, her voice
uncertain, Miriamne asked, "How are you, my lord?"

"I am not your lord. There is only one who is your lord. But
I am well enough." He turned his head up to the cistern's opening, as if seeking a shaft of light that had already passed earlier

in the day. His face, so recently pained, now seemed peaceful, as he stood with his eyes closed, chin up, neck exposed. Salomé saw his Adam's apple move as he swallowed with dry lips. He sighed and turned back to her.

"You have nothing to fear. The one you have seen in the wilderness will advocate for you. And you for him, later. You are forgiven."

Taken aback, Salomé stammered, "How do you know the man I saw? How do you know he said those words—that I am forgiven? Forgiven for what? What have I done? Have you lost your mind?"

He smiled at her. "Not what you have done, but what you will do. Don't fear. All will be well."

She bowed her head away from him, hands clenched, frightened by his words. Who was this man who spoke as if he knew the future, her future? Prophet or no, he should keep his beliefs to himself. Perhaps her mother was right to be so angry at him. Yet Salomé was drawn to look back at him. He now looked at Miriamne, as if he were finished with Salomé.

Salomé looked at her sister and saw her so taken, so pulled in by this man's presence, that it became instantly clear she was a third in the now intimate situation, as John turned his attention to the older girl. Miriamne moved closer to John, but withheld touching him, as she knew it was not acceptable. Even the two of them, as women, being alone in the presence of a man was irregular by Jewish standards. Still, he did not reject her closer presence, only turning his head slightly to look more at her shoulder than at her directly. She raised her hand, and he tilted his head away, as if expecting an unhurried blow; she paused, but pursued and held her hand above the crown of his head, hovering. In this way she ran her hand down, following the silhouette of his hair, then his shoulders, to his hips, finally letting her hand fall to her side. From the side Salomé could see her eyes tearing in earnest now, but as Miriamne leaned closer to John she began whispering to him. Even in the quiet of the dark circular space, Salomé could not hear what her sister was saying. Not wanting to disrupt their intimacy any further, and with a sense of foreboding at this ill-fated love that Herod would never sanction and the prophet could probably never fulfill, she quietly placed her feet on the ladder and began ascending, leaving them to the only seclusion they would likely ever know.

5

Later in the day

SALOMÉ TRUDGED back up the saddle of land, arms tucked tightly about her, slightly concerned she might be reprimanded for being out alone like a Greek woman if she were caught reentering the palace by herself. Since Herodias had given both her and Miriamne permission to visit John together, she would have a hard time explaining why she was returning by herself and where Miriamne was.

This time the refuse piles did not draw her attention, so lost was she in her thoughts about the situation. Looking up at the sky, she saw haze from the Dead Sea rising as if to engulf the fortress, extending its shroud. While the salt curtain of the sunken sea often streaked colorful sunsets, tonight promised a blood-hued sky. The moon had continued its climb, asserting itself, though still young and pallid.

So confused was Salomé's mind that she considered running into the desert to search for the man who had seemed to know so much, to have answers even though she had not asked questions of him at the time, a man . . . to be close to and touch. She wanted to part the layered air and take to it, free as a man in the wilderness wandering, not fettered by her woman's role, free to taste the dust, the desert sunsets and sunrises, to live purely and apart from the complications of the people in her life—her mother, her sister, her stepfather, this John. Her rising reluctance to don the mantle of adult relations urged her to fling off all that would be required of her now and in the future.

As she walked, she thought about her upcoming performance that evening. Beyond the town, to the north, dignitaries from Galilee had been making their way in caravans the last few days, intent on Herod's party. It was these people for whom Salomé would dance. Her love of the dance juxtaposed itself with her hatred for Herod, and the contrast galled her. Knowing her stepfather would ogle her, her sister would resent her, and her mother would respond God only knew how, she despaired under the spreading stain of red twilight. Her young mind couldn't sort through an ungraspable combination of her own umbrage, her mother's envy, and Miriamne's competition, all pressed against Herod's sexual attraction. As the last descended into her awareness, she stopped and rotated back to it. It made no sense; it couldn't fit. And yet she felt its peculiar oppression; it wasn't just from Herod she had sensed the cloying attraction. Nor, she anticipated, the men who would be at the party tonight. There was something odd in the way her mother responded to her these last several months, a closeness for which Salomé yearned but by which she was simultaneously revolted. Perhaps that was why she had lately been able only haltingly and in confusion to return to the warm, cozy memories of Mumma. Mumma was pushing her away but in some ways gripping her at the same time, and it was very confusing. Her face worked as she held an inner committee with herself. What Salomé wanted—could it matter what she wanted?—what she would do—would be to perform her best, focusing on the splendor of the dance and the dress. Her steps she knew; her body's motions, she knew. And so she decided: she would block out all else. She would not retreat to fuzzy childish memories. The dance was for neither Herod nor his guests, though they would be judging her. Nor was it to please her mother. Nor trump Miriamne. It was for her own pleasure, her own nourishment. She felt her legs steadying under her.

As she entered the fortress and wound her way through the halls and the central courtyard, crossing from the western to the eastern wing, passing the large sunken swimming pool onto whose surface a few olive leaves had drifted and floated, now stiff, she heard tense elevated voices from a room nearby. As she drew closer she recognized the tones and slunk nearer to eavesdrop, close enough to hear her mother and her stepfather arguing. She paused, a hand on the cool stone wall, outside.

"You have to keep him here? He is more than a thorn in our midst—he is—he is . . ." Unusually at a loss for words, Herodias screwed up her face and gestured with her hand to indicate her frustration. "It was not enough that he insulted us; now he threatens my daughter and you want to do nothing? What exactly is it that I have to do to convince you of this? To get your attention? Do I have to bring other men to my bed, since you seem to find it so cold lately, to get what I want?"

Herod snorted at his wife's threat. "Work out what you want for yourself. I doubt you want any men in your bed. If it's other men you do bring to your bed—or someone besides men—that's up to you. There's no need for killing here. He's a holy man, and I do not—I do not—care to harm him. I'll probably bring his zealots down upon my head as it is. The politics of it are tense. His words can't hurt us; you should be more selective about whose bones you want to sprinkle in the mountains of Moab. Your daughter is infatuated. It will pass."

"Imply what you like, you weak, vulgar fool. I see you looking at Salomé. You look at her so much that no one can help but notice. Do you think your guests won't notice? You embarrass yourself. If you are unable to contain yourself I'll take her and live apart from you. She's my daughter and she will go where I say and do as I say. She is marriageable, and I will lean on her standing. I would see her treated better than most women of this day and age. Don't even think about your plans. I would see her tethered to my own desires before I let you pin her to the pivot point of your lust."

"You've said it well! Such a way with words!" Herod sneered at her. "You should have been the captain of my guard. Then you would have all the control you want—except that you would be under my rule, still. There is no escaping this royal enclosure, Herodias. You wanted it; you got it. These are the confines of this arrangement we made. And I will determine both Salomé's and Miriamne's marriage arrangements."

"I understand the girls' marriages will be arranged. But I will work this out because it directly affects our standing." Here she paused. "I am surprised to hear that that is how you now see our marriage." If she could have seen her mother's face, Salomé would have sworn the woman exhaled ice as she said this.

"I rule." Herod's voice was stout, stubborn. "I say John rests with us indefinitely. I say your daughter will dance for me tonight. And you will join us." This last, however, he hissed at her.

So pounded the battering ram of their arguments. Salomé was weary of their altercations. She could feel the chill emanating from her mother, as if it would press through the very walls, though she could not see her face. She hadn't understood what her stepfather had insinuated about who her mother slept with, but not wanting to know any further, her hand dropped down in a whisper from the wall.

Moving off silently to her room, she locked in her heart the words she had heard. The afternoon's dying heat seeped in through window openings in the stone walls. Red-pink clouds gone to grey clustered into piles over the mountains of Moab, dissolving into the distance to lands she had never seen. The evening star had already risen, playing a duet with the moon's now pressing brightness. An air of tense expectancy hovered above the Dead Sea, as if the body of water itself could feel a coming storm as it braced for the onslaught of fresh penetrating droplets on its salt surface.

Salomé went into her room, her ears alert for the sound of Mumma's or Miriamne's footsteps in the hall, grateful that Herod's guests were staying in the other wing of the fortress. Silence settled over the interior. Feeling too young for all she was coming awake to, she contemplated the blue-green dress hanging empty of movement, then moved slowly to the garnet-encrusted trunk. "If Mumma doesn't think I should wear the blue, then maybe I'll wear the magenta," still wanting to please in some measure. She recalled her mother's selection of an ornately decorated and fringed, if too brilliantly colored, dress from one of their clothing sprees just as Salomé had begun dancing in earnest. Too tight around her breasts now, she wasn't sure if it would fit, and she wanted it to be comfortable enough so that she would have room to breathe when she moved.

Fingers feeling coolness as she played them over the trunk, she admired the intricate ivory carving, remembering the look on her mother's face when she had presented her daughter with the gift. It wasn't a look she had seen often: a soft anticipation, paying close attention to Salomé's face for her reaction, running her own hands over it as she passed it to her, telling her they would share the box, she keeping it for Salomé until she was old enough to take possession of it and be responsible for its care. Within a year she had given it to her daughter. It was a costly item, intended to hold the most precious of belongings. Salomé wanted the trunk to last for years so that she would have it long after she had moved away from her mother and was living with her own husband and children. But then she thought of the man from the desert . . . Casting her mind into the future she wondered if she would meet him again.

At the sight of the red dress, a discomfiting mix of love and revulsion toward her mother swept through her. Lifting the dress delicately out of the trunk and backing toward the bed to lay it out, she glanced at the blue-green dress and marveled at the contrast of the red's self-announcement. Clearly the red was too small for her now; she knew she had outgrown it. Still, silver beading that she liked very much ornamented its waist. She placed her hands on the fine fabric. Then, in a sudden thrust, she picked it up, ripped it apart at the breast, crumpled it, and flung it at the wall. Squatting at the foot of the bed she covered her mouth with her hands, eyes wide at what she had done. Then she began crying, her shoulders caving in. She had torn the last shreds of what she supposed were happy childhood memories and thrown them blindly at her mother's disingenuousness and malnourishment of her daughters.

Crying filled the quiet space as Salomé wiped the river running out of her nose and eyes on the sleeve of her tunic. With deliberation she removed her outer garment, then blew her nose hard one more time on it before piling it next to her. Half-expecting her commotion to draw the attention of her mother or sister or a servant, she stole a glance at the doorway, but the descending evening continued layering its air like silt sifting down to hush more deeply all her young emotions.

Standing, she went to the window overlooking the rampart toward the cistern she had gone to earlier in the day. In the dusk she saw Miriamne making her way back toward the fortress, head down and cloaked. Good Lord, had she been with John all that time? Salomé wondered. She should have stayed to wait for Miriamne. The guards must have separated the man and young woman at some point. Had Miriamne gone to the town, or into the wilderness, like Salomé had? Surely nothing unseemly would have passed between the prophet and the girl . . .

Miriamne moved unevenly, one hip swinging ahead of the other, and Salomé felt the gap between them widen even as she watched her sister with a maturing gaze that now missed nothing. Her sister seemed small in the swallowing twilight of the surrounding desert, fragile within its vast wasteland. Looking down on Miriamne she felt a surge of power, as if she were now the elder, selected for loveliness by her stepfather and chosen by her mother for an unspoken part she would play. Like a performer balancing on the tremulous ball of her mother's unreliable affection, she juggled in her mind what to do with Miriamne's secret to which she imagined she was now privy. Would her mother want to use Miriamne's affections in some way, as she wanted to use Salomé's looks? She knew her mother was aware of Miriamne's interest in John, but she didn't believe Mumma knew the extent to which the two were folding into one another's hearts. She see-sawed between exposing her sister and protecting her from her mother's maneuverings.

Salomé turned back to the torn red dress and stuffed it under the bed. Next she took the blue-green one down from where it hung and laid it on the bed. Hearing movement out in the hall, she turned to see a servant named Susanna grasp the curtain to her room and hesitantly ask if she needed help in dressing for the dinner dance.

"I will dress myself, Susanna, thank you."

"The evening has come upon us quickly, your Highness, and the guests have gathered. If you will not be present for the meal, would you like me to bring you something so that you will not be dancing on an empty stomach?"

"That will be fine, Susanna, but something light—just some olives and bread. And some water, please."

"As you wish." She disappeared back down the hall.

Salomé shed her clothing in a heap and went to stand at the window, feeling the breeze feathering across her young skin. Leaning out, she looked into the distant wilderness, yearning for its space and freedom. Then with a sigh, she turned back into the room. She went to the sea-colored dress, raised her arms, and slipped the sensuous silk over her head as the skirt slid in a shimmer down her body. Next she fastened tightly about her hips a triangle-shaped scarf with hundreds of tiny silver coins sewn into it. Topless now, her shoulders and clavicle broad and striking, she flung her head upside down and brushed out the strands of her long hair, giving it body. When she righted herself, she took the tight-fitting cupped top layer of the costume and walked over to the mirrored silver sheet on the wall, hanging the top upon it. Salomé looked into her own eyes, ignoring her bare breasts while enjoying this freedom of dressing alone, being able to simply feel her own body without also having to be aware of the reactions of others—whether the women dressing her or the men ogling her. To live in a world in which she inspired no response whatsoever—how freeing would that be, she wondered? Turning her head to the right, then the left, she picked up a small pearlized case of kohl-blackening with its applicator brush and began lining her eyes, drawing the brush out to exaggerate their almond shape. Above each eyebrow she painted a series of dots designed to draw more attention, then on her lips she painted a salve-like substance dyed with pomegranates, dotting some of it on her cheeks after mixing it with a lotion to spread it evenly. She had always thought putting on this highlighting coloration made her face too exaggerated, but her mother told her men seemed to love it, so she would acquiesce to their desires. She knew keenly in what way the dance was for herself, and in what way it was for the men. And for the envious women. None of it, she reiterated for herself, none of it was for Mumma.

Watching herself in the mirror she raised her arms and wound them like snakes about her head. Her hips followed suit in a seemingly unending circular undulation. Closing her eyes she felt the dance move through her body; this was the dance for herself. It was as if someone or something moved through her, as if there were invisible hands on her waist sliding her about, and she was simply following. She slowed, lifted the top from the mirror, slid her arms through it, and in a contortion managed to tie its strings in the back and at her neck to secure it in place, pushing her breasts around until the top was securely situated and would remain that way throughout the dance, even though it looked as though her breasts might burst from the low cut at any moment.

She particularly enjoyed the illusion this top provided. Next she retrieved a blue-green gossamer scarf, wrapped it around her throat, letting it flow down her back, then picked it up and tucked each side of it into her skirt at the hips so that her hips were even more exaggerated. With one final glance in the mirror, she went and stood at the window again, as if to present herself to the vast silence before she went down to the gathering people.

Night had descended. Stars glittered on a velvet blue cloak cast over the mountains. Stillness hung, pensive, with the jostle of the beginning party below barely denting the night's motionlessness. Herod must be over his tantrum by now. Salomé thought of the man in the subterranean prison whose only view this night would be a deepening indigo circle of sky above him. Was he at peace? She thought of her sister lying awake thinking of him, blinking up at the ceiling, but him falling off to sleep secure amidst his uncertain prison and likely thinking of just his God. Feeling very alone, she tapped out the toe of her foot, turned her delicate ankle, shook her hips quickly to hear the tinkle of the coins, then with trepidation decided to descend to her performance. She moved to the trunk her mother had given her, opened it, and removed from it a set of finger cymbals to complete her costume. Next, she slowly slipped a ring on the finger of each hand and added some bangles to her wrists and one higher up on her arm. Reluctantly bedecked, though hoping she could please, she moved out the door to go below.

6

Evening

SALOMÉ GLIDED through the lamplit hallways, jingling softly, passing flowing servants who turned down sheets for guests and placed bowls of hair oil on each bedside table in a choreography of concern for their betters. Moving past the pool, still under the now black sky, she glanced in the direction of the steam baths. Most likely her mother was in the steam room rather than participating in Herod's dinner. Lately she had been avoiding meals with the family, taking food in her own quarters, and Salomé could not help but wonder if Miriamne had developed the habit of not eating from observing her mother's loudly silent protest.

Salomé paused, her heart beating like a bird's wings at her neck, her breath coming shorter. Never for any performance had she been this anxious. She stood cemented for a few moments, unable to go either forward or retreat to her room. She knew that not to perform was unacceptable, but every breath that pushed her life forward into the future right now made her want to tear herself from the fabric of her family and run back into the wilderness looking for the man in whose presence she had felt such deep momentary peace. After a few minutes of this frozenness, her scanning mind found a temporary outlet: she would go and find Miriamne, who must have returned by now. Briefly she looked toward the tepidarium, thinking of going to find her mother, but rejected the idea, feeling only a cold breeze coming from its direction. Miriamne it was.

Gathering about her the brilliant kaleidoscope of colored fabric, she trotted back upstairs. Her feet stumbled on one stair, but continued, taking her body in the direction of Miriamne's room. Hesitating only briefly, she entered without waiting for a reply from Miriamne.

Head down, hands cradled into one another in her lap, Miriamne sat on the floor, eyes now dry. The air in the room lay oppressive and there was a cloth drawn across the window, though Salomé didn't know why. Lately, half the time she had ignored her sister, and the other half she had worried about her, feeling impotent to dislodge her from the malaise she seemed to have fallen into with the reduction in eating. Now her concern came fully alive.

"Salomé!" Miriamne looked up at her sister, wan but surprised as well. She gasped. "You look so beautiful . . ."

Salomé settled on the floor opposite Miriamne, her delicate robes spreading around her, but she felt a little sheepish as her cleavage tilted toward her sister who had not been asked to show off her body to the men waiting below. Miriamne, however, seemed lost in her own world. Salomé wanted desperately to have her sister to herself, right now, as if their growing bodies and moods had never changed them, as if Mumma had never been between them. Even if only for a few moments of security the younger wanted to touch the elder, to calm herself before going back downstairs to what she knew she must execute. She drew her toes in underneath her and crossed her arms over her chest to cover the breasts that seemed to threaten to create forever a divide of maturity and womanhood between the two girls. The indolent air hung between them, and Salomé knew she would have to exert herself in an effort to come into Miriamne's puzzling world if she were to derive any reassurance for herself before going back downstairs. "I'm nervous . . . I was hoping I could talk to you before I went down there."

A small smile at the corner of her mouth, Miriamne slowly blinked long eyelashes at her sister. Salomé sensed her coming up out of a torpor.

"You're nervous? Confident, gorgeous you?"

Salomé felt the weight shift, as if her sister knew she held Salomé's vulnerability cupped in her hand. She waited, with some mistrust, to see how Miriamne would handle the temporarily awarded power. Miriamne seemed to lightly enjoy her ascendancy at this point, glancing away from her sister and toward the window, but then she seemed to shed her status just as readily. She sighed and focused back in on Salomé.

"What can I say to you that will calm you? You have to do what you have to do. I can't do it for you; anyway, I'm glad I don't have to. I'm grateful Herod chose you, not me. Tonight you are the darling; may you never be the scapegoat, or suffer notoriety in any way from this performance," she added enigmatically.

Salomé frowned but she didn't know how to respond to this last comment. "What are you thinking about?" was the best she could manage.

"You will marry soon. Perhaps to one of these guests from the north, from Herod's contacts in Galilee. One of those men downstairs. Certainly not your heart's desire: we're not permitted that. And in any case, the men we want may not want us," she added sadly.

"Why not?" challenged Salomé. "Why can't we have what we want?" she asked, beating against the fetters of her existence, and in her own self-involvement missing the implication that John had rejected Miriamne.

"Because even if it were acceptable for us to choose whom we marry, you know Mumma would hold sway over our choices. Herod thinks he'll choose, but you know perfectly well Mumma will be the one who decides. Who cares what you want? Think about it, Salomé. You must do what is best for all of us. Do you think I haven't dreamed of living with John? His hands"—and here Salomé saw Miriamne's eyes go distant—"his hands. Have you noticed them? No, no, I know his nails are ragged and not groomed like those of the men downstairs. But I don't care about that. In my dreams I feel his chest against my body." Salomé's eyes got wider. "I feel the heat coming off his body, and his eyes burn into me. He looks at me only, you know. His eyes long for me, and our souls are joined. I can feel it. And when I look up at him, in his embrace, I see his neck—his long neck and throat." She laughed a light, thin laugh. "I run my finger along his neck. His chin tucks just over my head as he pulls me closer to him. Even in my dreams I feel this, Salomé, and it's so vivid, it's so real, I feel our coming together must happen. But then I wake and I remember who I am under Herod's roof. And under Mumma's sway." She looked up, pleading, at Salomé, then glanced over her shoulder at the temporarily curtained window, placed as if to keep her urges from flying out unbidden.

Salomé sat contemplatively playing with a ring on her right hand. As a wife to a king or man of high standing of some sort she would have this silver and gold and jewels and more. She would be able to provide for her mother regardless of what happened to Herod; her mother would never suffer the fate of a widow. But Salomé knew she wouldn't have the passion in her marriage at which Miriamne hinted. Still, her sister's desire for the man John squeezed the room smaller, as if it were more obsession, and Salomé began to feel there was no space for her to breathe in the close quarters. Wasn't love supposed to create more space than it took away?

Rising on unsteady legs, Miriamne got up and went to the window and pulled the fabric aside. As the moonlight angled off the tile floor, Salomé realized she had just vanished in her sister's mind. Slowly, she got up; pausing at the curtained doorway, she looked back in hopes of catching her sister's awareness once more, wishing she could have found the solace she had come seeking. Instead, she realized she was alone as she turned, sighed, and went out.

"Dance for yourself, Salomé, not for them," she heard Miriamne say softly, her back to her sister, as the curtain fell heavily.

Salomé recognized as she drifted sadly down the hallway that for much longer than she realized she had been content with the feeling of half-satisfaction and half-love. As if she should be fulfilled with only partial affection in her life, she began walking, intent on making in her mind the transition from a childhood belief in security and love to the perpetually starved love of adulthood. It was a cold reality at which Miriamne hinted, but still Salomé was unwilling to settle for such a parsimonious existence. If she could have neither the love of her rightful father, nor that of a mother who was mysteriously unavailable to her, nor the true and intimate affection of a man of high standing, then why could she not have the complete and engulfing love of the man in the wilderness? As she walked the halls seemed to echo with the thoughts in her head. She descended the stairs again without awareness she was doing so, then found herself going past the steam baths and into the open space of the courtyard.

The space around her was silent, as if the night had drawn out all the servants from the area and toward the dining hall in the triclinium, from which she could now hear condensed sounds of conviviality. Herod's great wind had sucked all life into the gathering for the night. Salomé paused under the stars of the courtyard open to the sky, then glanced down the hall into the room that held the rare birds. It too was silent now, the winged living things stilled for the evening, in obedient anticipation of the fabric that would soon be placed over each cage by the servants. Not a flutter or twitter escaped, and Salomé used the quiet to calm her own heart. She drove all thoughts out of her head, moved her life force into the center of her body, then glided down the hall to the triclinium past a miniature sunken garden of tamarisks, oleanders, vines, poplars, willows, and some branchy growth with thorns unfamiliar to her.

Brushing past a servant who exited the dining hall and bowed to her, she made her entrance into the brilliance of Herod's party. Oil lamp sconces dotted the walls and lit the room in a hon-eyed glow. Low-lying tables surrounded by pillows on the floor were set with thin fine pottery and overflowed with flasks of wine, bowls of grapes, dishes of hummus and plates of flatbread and ol-ives marinated in rosemary. In the center of the room a small boy clad in a patchwork of red, yellow, and orange cloth performed a silent series of moves with a hoop and a small long-haired dog, as a few of the women in the gathering watched him, all smiles, some genuine. Those women, and a few around them, turned to stare at Salomé as she entered, the smiles leaving as, she assumed, they took in her figure and her clothing. A haze of smoldering aromatic herbs hung in the air, giving the room a gauzy look, as if to cloak the deceptions and small intrigues of the minds in the room, but Salomé possessed a sense of cutting through this veil as she entered. She glanced toward Herod and saw the drunken look in his eye as he turned his head to her. Dipping her head slightly, fixing him with her gaze then withdrawing it when she decided to rather than flinching under his stare, she moved to the end of a table two tables away from him and sat as a servant approached her and filled the cup in front of her.

Salomé felt with the inborn sense of being stared at that the flushed sunkenness of her stepfather's eyes stayed on her, lingering at her breasts. As if through the din she could hear his mouth close and swallow while he tried to contain the lascivi-ous thoughts stealing from his eyes to his groin, she sat very still and looked up at him again under hooded lashes, her ringed fin-gers long and splayed out in front of her on the table. Standing straight up, Herod blindly fumbled his wine goblet down on the table behind him, then turned to face her directly. Salomé curved her soft pink cheek to the side slightly, as if to gently deflect his intense scrutiny even while vaguely acknowledging it.

A drunken courtier with a too-big swath of purple silk crashed into Herod, causing the tetrarch to curse and turn away momentarily from Salomé. She saw the man apologize, head bowing several times down to his knees, then saw Herod's interest dart back to her as if to pin her down with the claw of his eyes. Trying to recover his hold on the great brawl of a party he had initiated to celebrate his petty oppression, even as things seemed to be spinning out of his authority, he floundered backwards into a chair and surveyed the landscape of people around him.

"I wonder if he sees what I see?" mused Salomé. Drunken statues, frozen yet breathing and moving, inebriated courtiers and wealthy men and women from the highest ranks of society cluttered the room, crowding out the pure space into which she intended to take her dance. Miriamne was right: she should dance for herself, not those preening and jockeying before her. It was only her anger toward Herod that could propel her initially past their infection. They seemed to her like colorful but diseased birds in their own cages of prominence and power, blanketed by the wine they consumed. She also considered that perhaps there was a connection between her rising fury and her own desire for power. She could clearly see the connection between fury and power linking her mother and Herod; but what she had not noticed before was the extent to which the clutch for power existed in relationships all around her, in the underlying civility with which people covered their grasping fear. Was it possible that this was her mother's underlying motivation in her daughters' lives? That her mother vied for power with her daughter as well as with her husband? Perhaps it had more to do with her mother than with either herself or Miriamne. Or Herod, for that matter. The absurdity of these thoughts swept through Salomé with a quick violence, dismissed as readily as they had flown in; they were too complex for her to hold for any length of time.

For relief, turning her thoughts to Miriamne, she supposed that she and her elder sister had long ago given up their fledgling efforts at both freedom and supremacy when it became clear that Salomé was the favored and more blessed daughter. But perhaps Miriamne saw it differently. Maybe that was what Miriamne's contention was with her food intake: simply a vying for power with Herodias, and maybe with God, as well. But this thought dead-ended too, and brought Salomé no solace this time. So she forced herself to find some joy in her contemplation of her sister. At least she had seen a purity in Miriamne's intensity of affection for John. And the clarity in the face of the man Salomé had bumped into in the desert—that was on a different scale altogether.

Yet here, in the melee of dignitaries ornately jeweled and brilliantly festooned, as she listened in on conversations, she saw manipulation in the faces of the women, their fingers twirling in their elaborate hairstyles as they stirred their relationships in conversation, along with a calculating deception in the refined gestures and sickly sweet words of obsequious men speaking honey to get into Herod's good graces. How could she maneuver in such a gutter of human intrigue? Was there truth behind anyone's eyes? How could she navigate the intricacies of adulthood without Mumma instructing her? And what good was Mumma's instruction if in the end it had its genesis in the vying for power with her anyway? The thoughts immobilized her, stringing her up as if she were next on the line for the carnivorous hawk.

Salomé turned to see Herod reclining against an intricately carved ivory-backed wooden chair covered with a purple cushion. One of his shoulders was higher than the other, one leg stuck straight out as he lounged, leering again at her. In his be-ringed hand he held an oversized silver goblet from which slopped droplets of wine as he shifted, eyes flitting around him to see if anyone else was watching him observe his stepdaughter, hoping against hope that no one was noticing when in fact the attraction was easy to detect. Salomé followed his eyes, watched them look over the clustered heads of men and women talking, then settle in a far corner on a darkened doorway.

As she followed where he looked, she was surprised to see Miriamne half-hidden outside the door looking on, entranced by the spectacle in the room. Confusion again stalled Salomé as she wondered what her sister intended. But the unbeautiful daughter remained concealed, simply observing quietly. Though Salomé would have preferred her sister not watch the inevitable performance, she recognized she could not keep her sister from seeing her. As best she could she tried to ignore the shadowy presence at the other end of the room.

Suddenly a shrill, piercing screech stabbed the hubbub and the room bled into silence. As all faces turned to locate the sound, Salomé noticed the prized hawk Herod had wanted to show off, perched on a branch-stand in the opposite corner of the triclinium near some tables laden with a luscious mound of ruby-red pomegranate kernels. Herod frowned in the direction of the bird, then turned left and right, smiling broadly at his guests, looking as if he would take off the head of the servant closest to him if someone didn't gratify the bird. The servant scuttled over toward the offending display, reached into a nearby silver bucket to retrieve some rodent bodies, and fed a few to the bird. Women nearby lifted their chins in disgust, the look of rising bile painting their faces under their careful powdering, while the men stayed silent momentarily longer. Some digested the metaphor, looking to Herod with wariness in their eyes; then they turned back to the conversations they had been having to gulp down more red wine, as if to turn their muddled thoughts to what they could get at the end of the night of feasting. Salomé could only wonder if she were about to be fed to the crowd in a similar fashion.

Herod turned to a troupe of musicians nearby and struck his hands together for them to play. There were lyres of different shapes and ranges, as well as an arghul, the double-reeded instrument of two different pipe lengths, along with double flutes and drums. The music began to sway Salomé's body, pulling her in, and she felt torn in two, as if she would be betrayed by her own seductive art—the killing inertia of resistance stealing over her even as she felt the pulse of percussion taking her body almost in spite of herself. It was as if the music provided for her a life of its own, as if the music alone could free and transport her. She looked over to Miriamne, but there was no help to be found there, and Herodias was still absent. If Salomé began dancing, winding her hands above her head to highlight her breasts, if she pointed her toe out to the side from beneath her skirt to show off her leg, a lascivious man from one of Herod's underlings might stop his guzzling and decide he wanted to take her home with him—to steal her away from her mother, displace her on account of her flesh—and yet the dance had always and only been for herself, a freedom in the movement. As if poised on a cliff, windmilling her arms in large circles to regain balance and prevent herself from falling off into the abyss of others' claims, she worked to regain her carriage.

The music's sweep won. Slowly she rose from her cushion. As she moved to the center of the floor, gliding to position herself before her stepfather, the people swarming the floor melted away from her, leaving her space to move. The lead musician glanced over his shoulder, turned around more fully, even as he kept time, leading the rest of the players. With a waggle of his fingers he changed the tempo of the tune to one he knew would particularly suit the young dancer. She smiled in his direction and momentarily felt she had an ally. He too loved the rhythm, the bend, the life in the music. What he chose was a beat that caused her to thrust out her hips, coins jingling, the bunched fabric at her hips jumping to life, accentuating her curves. First her hips led, then her feet, and the space around her grew larger, people quieting, setting down their wine, pushing aside their food and taking their seats. Men smiled; women stilled, envy and comparison sweeping through them. With each thrust of her feet the onlookers' eyes flashed from the rings on her toes, to her hips, which responded to keep her forward motion in balance. The ivory arc of her belly undulated first slowly, then faster, causing Herod to gasp with pleasure and clap. It seemed he might leap up out of his chair to come over to her. Salomé flowed toward him, taking the diaphanous scarf from around her neck, twirling around with it, making it a ghost partner as she first veiled her face, then exposed it. Her eyelids batted languorously in the direction of the onlookers as she circled the room, speeding up the thrusting of her feet and hips, then slowing to rise and fall as if writhing in pleasure under a man she had not yet known. She flung out the scarf, but holding on at the last moment she retrieved it, shrouding her head and body, bending into herself; the crowd stilled and Herod leaned forward. As if outside herself, she burst upwards and outwards, increasing the frenzy of her circular hip and belly motions, the jingle of the coins growing more intense, building to a climax. With miniature rapid footsteps she flew about the room, carrying her to the freedom of her soul in the movement of the dance, the brightness in her eyes betraying her joy at the flight. As she circled, she barely registered that Miriamne had disappeared from the doorway, leaving not even the breath of her shadow.

The leader slowed the music, the drum beat took over, dreamy and dripping with slow sensuality. Salomé's arms rose slowly above her head, snakes rising from steam. As they descended about her, caressing her own body, she went down upon her knees, arched her back, and gradually shook her shoulders to the floor with her arms still making waves in the air. Her cleavage and white neck were fully exposed as her arced body defied the pull of the ground and she curved, breasts jutting up toward the ceiling. Herod melted in his chair, sliding down farther in it, his mouth again hanging open, thoroughly besotted by his stepdaughter's performance. For a moment Salomé was pulled out of her reverie and began to peel her shoulders up from the floor as she resurrected herself, feeling as if her mother stood in the doorway where Miriamne had been, looking at her. But when she turned, pivoting around the yet-moving arms above her head, there was no one there in the door. She dissolved back into the motion, which began at her fingertips this time and shimmied through her neck, then her arms and next her torso, then down through her groin and out through her feet, grounding the stirring that offered to levitate her out of her body. This time the coins tinkled faintly, masking a hidden eagerness, hinting at greater and deeper passion, inviting her audience to take flight in their minds at where this body escape could lead. By all appearances the tease was nearly skewering Herod. Salomé glanced over her shoulder at her stepfather and felt the queer sensation of the influence she held over him at this point, an influence she had not sought but that he now dumped in her lap. She scarcely knew what she could do with it. Perhaps she did need Mumma after all to educate her in the sway women held, even against their best selves. But she doubted her mother would be willing to share her secrets. Pushing aside unwelcome thought, she again let the music sweep her, taking her to the pure state that nonetheless now seemed complicated by this awareness of her growing mind and body. Gradually the music wound down, and so did she, spent, as she folded herself under the scarf, crumpling before the tetrarch.

"Marvelous!" howled Herod. As if remembering himself, he lurched up out of his chair and this time lunged his torso toward Salomé, his hands gripping the arms of his throne, though his lower half seemed glued to his seat, made impotent to move by the consumption of too much wine.

A general huzzah followed the cessation of music, men calling for more, women turning even their mesmerized gazes from the young woman who had set on fire the room before them, unwilling to acknowledge the force of beauty bowing before them. They knew that not even with the most exquisite face-painting, the most expensive jewels and silks, the most outlandish high hairstyles could they approximate what Salomé had just presented; there was an ardor that exuded from her as an internal unity, drawing all energy in a vortex toward her. Without seeking power, she alone in the room possessed it. When she stopped, her audience reeled, bereft. Sucking breath to find life within themselves, they turned sycophantic selves to one another again, seeking other lifeblood.

Herod had managed to uproot himself. Holding up his goblet, wavering on his pegs, he raised both arms high. His royal tunic was splattered with juices from meat and fruits, and bits of bread nested in his beard.

He staggered toward his stepdaughter, who was still crouched on the floor, masked under the lake of gossamer sea-green scarf. The faintest hint of breath fluttered the edge of the sheer fabric, indicating she was still living.

Too loudly, Herod stood before her and declared to the room, "You are magnificent. You have performed better than I could have asked for. I will reward you with anything you want, even up to half my kingdom," and here he looked around the room smiling, to catch the startled looks on the faces of his guests as they heard the magnanimous pronouncement.

Salomé remained still. Her chest heaved from exertion. Between catching her breath and feeling the ponderous weight of Herod in her sphere, she could not move. Now, his offer hanging on the air before her, she froze in earnest. He was offering her his kingdom, his power, that very thing of which she had so recently become aware. Her mind flooded, overwhelmed. Her fingers curled around the edges of the scarf she held about her, and she pulled it more tightly about her, as if to withdraw like a turtle in its shell. But surely this was not what Mumma would have had her do . . .

"Salomé!" Herod barked at her. With her stalling she threatened to make him look like an idiot before his guests. "Salomé! I offer you my kingdom, up to half of it. Anything you would like. What would you like? Salomé!" The desperation in his voice mounted. Fury, the flip side of his authority, began to work his facial expression in spite of himself, though he was on display before all of his guests. He planted his feet more firmly and crouched down, breathing on the scarf she held about her as if to penetrate it. Seeing the rings on one of her clutched hands he scrabbled for her, reaching to pull her up with him. Wrested onto her feet, she stood, still hunched, terrified before him. Just because she could begin to understand that power and control and fury were the front and back ends of the same animal did not mean she was capable of knowing what to do with the information. She looked at him wide-eyed, all intelligence flown from her mind. Her shoulders collapsed and the fear on her face echoed in his as puzzlement, he to whom power was second nature. Her inability to comprehend what he was offering her, and why, appeared to irritate him, but her mind stayed clouded and she began bowing before him, then she asked to be excused.

"Your Highness, forgive me, I am stunned by the generosity of your offer . . ." she filled the air with empty phrases. "I shall return momentarily. Please know how grateful I am. Please, I'll return . . ." and her words trembling before her, she turned and ran from the room, hearing the huzzahing pick up and a guffaw burst from Herod.

Salomé stumbled back toward the steam baths, dully hoping to find Miriamne to retrieve her from this uncomfortable dream. Her sister was nowhere in sight, and Salomé's face squinted with her discomfiture. Mumma would know what to ask for. Mumma would advise her. Her trot slowed as she clutched her skirts about her and wrapped the scarf around her entire body to cover herself.

She burst into the baths and sought out her mother.

"Mumma! Mumma!"

A servant pointed toward the tepidarium. "She's just finishing up in there, your Highness."

Salomé moved through the small humid room, steam dripping off columns and stone benches set at the side of the room, which had piped-in hot water. She exited through a door into the pool area, glancing at its placid water. Still cloudy in her thinking, she believed she was right to seek out her mother's advice on Herod's offer. How could she possibly make the decision herself? Mumma would know what to do.

She went through the last entryway, coming into the slightly cooler tepidarium, which was used as an in-between room so that the body would not be too shocked by the transition from the steam room to the cool waters of the pool. The steam baths kept a woman's face young and moist, Herodias contended, and she spent much time here. She had indeed chosen to be here this night rather than attend Herod's party, as Salomé had suspected, without thinking why.

Herodias was stepping out of the lukewarm water and rose, naked, before her daughter. Salomé stood uncomfortably before her, seeing her mother drip, her nipples pointing rigid and dark on breasts that hung like late summer gourds. The stark line between the patch of hair between her legs and her long fleshy thighs seemed vaguely threatening, as if it could swallow her daughter's thinly clothed and newly grown sensuality. They stood facing one another, Herodias's face hard. Salomé assumed that because of the intrusion her mother had not immediately reached for a linen with which to cover herself. But as if wanting to bludgeon her daughter with her own sexuality, Herodias stood, frightful in her austere nakedness.

Then, arching her eyebrows, she reached down to a nearby bench to pull a cloth about her. "What is it?"

Despite the moisture in the room, Salomé's mouth had dried up. "Mumma," she whispered.

"Well?"

"*Abba*—I mean, Herod—has told me to ask for anything I want. I danced for him. He liked it." The simple sentences of a young girl were all she could manage. "He wants me to ask for whatever I want, even up to half his kingdom . . . I don't know what he means. I don't know what I should ask for. I don't know what I want. What do I want?" the girl, thrust too soon into adulthood, asked the woman before her.

As if the act of dumping the question in her mother's now bound and clothed lap had freed her, Salomé stood helplessly, awaiting an answer.

A slow curl spread across Herodias's mouth.

The mother came alongside her daughter and clasped her hand firmly, leading her back into the pool area, head down. Behind that wall of which Salomé had so recently become aware, calculations and manipulations that Salomé could not begin to touch moved her mother's face. Then, as if having hit on the solution, done with her daughter, she dropped—flung, almost—Salomé's hand from hers.

"You will ask . . ." she paused, sucking in her breath, seeming to double-check with herself internally, "you will ask for the head of John the Baptist." Her teeth showed as her lips tightened across her mouth, and as if dotting her pronouncement, she finished with, "On the finest of our silver plates." She bit off the last sentence.

Salomé, stunned, felt the words penetrate her chest. Then, the bitter taste of her stomach rising, she lunged toward the pool and vomited. As she grasped its edges and heaved again she perceived her mother standing over her. She looked up over her shoulder, her eyes pleading with her mother.

"But Mumma . . . Miriamne . . ."

"What about Miriamne?"

"She loves him! How can you ask this?" Her voice whimpered. "What has the prophet done to you that you should want . . . this?" Rage boiled up now to replace her bile at her mother's despicable demand. Again she turned to the pool, one last spewing splashing into the now-clouded water.

"What—Miriamne's little heart throbbing toward the holy man? She is sick with love. You will do as I say. He has insulted your stepfather and me, and I tire of his continued existence here. He takes up space, and our food, and time from the guards. But I don't need to explain it to you. You have a choice to make: heed my request, or your sister's pitiful yearnings. Besides, you can't go back to that fox of a stepfather with nothing to request of him, and look the fool." Again she raised an eyebrow, but did not offer Salomé anything on which to wipe her mouth.

"But what about what I wa . . ."

"Do it!" Herodias screeched at her daughter, eyes black fire, hair shiny and wet against her long neck.

Salomé stumbled to her feet, the coins jangling as she did. She exited the room, back through the blasting humid heat of the steam room, and stumbled out into the courtyard. Crying, despair propelling her forward, she wiped her nose on her scarf, as her feet faltered her back in the direction of the triclinium. A hot, dry wind, countering the moist air of the baths, blew through the hallway that seemed to endlessly telescope in the distance from her. She moved mindlessly, pulling the skimpy scarf about her, seeking comfort but finding none in its thin threads and milky fabric.

As she passed the rare bird room she paused and stood, too dull to move one way or the other. Wavering there she heard a small, colorful jewel twittering, the single melodic trill of one bird in particular catching her ear. It was enough to impel her forward as if the movement came from beyond her, so she slid into the room and crouched in a corner, huddling, looking at the cages of colorful birds before her. Staring blankly at them, she was momentarily distracted from her numbing misery.

Each specimen, regardless of the native habitat from which it had been extracted and captured, had been provided for scrupulously according to its needs. Most often they survived, though sometimes they did fail to thrive in captivity, at which time all the other birds seemed to grow silent. There was the purple Swamphen, which was popular with the Romans, sporting a red beak and mask and indigo coat, about the size of a chicken. For the most part it had a quiet call but now and then would let out a raucous shriek. The Cream-Colored Courser was a desert inhabitant with long legs and wings and a down-curved bill, and there was a Laughing Dove, a tame bird with rich chestnut-red underwings and black spotting on its throat. That one seemed to do all right being alone, and since all it did all day was eat seeds and grains it had grown quite fat. But Salomé's favorite, apart from the Green Bee-Eater, was the Barn Owl in delicate white with a heart-shaped face, black-ringed eyes, and brown speckled wings. All but one of them remained silent, simply hopping about in their cages and tilting their heads to observe her.

She had been flung between one rage-filled parent into the grasping arms of another and was now a pawn in their game of swiping. Dull as her mind ached right now, she knew Herod would not want this demand from Herodias; he would reject it, and Salomé feared being batted back to her mother to amend the request. Once again her mind took flight for relief, going back to a time when she and Miriamne had run from stall to stall in the market, fingers playing over the intricate weave of some styles of baskets they had never seen before. The woman who had made them and sold them was richly dressed in a deeply hued thick cotton tunic that highlighted the rosiness of her cheeks. Her heavy, mysterious eyebrows and eyelashes balanced the thick dark curls of hair that lay on her shoulders, and she had a subterranean laugh that made Salomé and Miriamne pause, as Salomé wondered about the happiness of home that shone through the woman's eyes. Surely both she and Miriamne could have such happiness and be so obviously well loved, finding husbands who filled their souls and made them laugh so. Surely it was not too late—Salomé could run in the opposite direction, not going to Herod with the odious request, but seeking out Miriamne. They could pack up some items and run to the cistern, pull out John, and the three of them would go seek the other man in the wilderness. By the time Herod and Herodias had figured out that Salomé had gone to neither of them she and Miriamne could be safely away into the hills of Moab by the light of the moon . . .

She paused and looked at the one tiny trilling bird in its cage, the one that had not silenced itself when she had come in. Looking at the bird on its perch in the small gilded cage, the lack of time for her plan pressed against her heart. The realities of the childish notion to run away struck at her young adult heart. Herodias might take her time, but in her blood thirst she would want to see the product of her desire; she would want to witness John's naked neck and head herself. She would be alerted to the fact that Salomé had defied her. Salomé felt a cold sweat break out on her face as she imagined her mother's wrath on discovering her daughter's defiance. This defiance was as foreign to Salomé as the lands from which these birds had been captured. It split her from her mother. As for Herod's reaction, Salomé could not begin to conceive of it either way, given the clouds in her mind—whether she came to him with the abominable request, or whether she escaped.

But how would they live in the wilderness? The man, John, was said to have existed on locusts and wild honey, but Salomé and Miriamne had only known the finest food in their lives. They had never wanted, for either clothing or food or water, and the reality of a life of deprivation began to sink into Salomé's quickly retreating resolve. The two girls had been served their entire lives, and now she could hardly conceive of the prophet serving either one of them. And then of course he was a prophet. His life had not been dedicated to caring for a woman up to this point, unless one considered Israel his bride—at this she smirked—and she did not believe he would begin to care for even Miriamne in the way the girl had hoped. No doubt the other holy man in the wilderness would be the same: a life pledged to an entire people, with no distinction made for women, or a specific woman, apart from anyone else. Salomé began to cry, and she pushed her back harder, repeatedly, into the cool stone wall, not sure which way to turn.

Then, her thoughts ricocheting back to hope, she imagined that surely John could at least help them survive in the wilderness until they reached a town in which they could find support. He must be grateful to her if she saved his life! Salomé bargained in her mind. The alternative was simply too gruesome—she could not return to it in her mind, so she looked pleadingly at the small bird and ran her fingers through her hair. Miriamne would be forever grateful to her if she resisted her mother and did not do this thing. But Miriamne was weaker than she was, and Salomé wondered how her sister would walk in the wilderness, even if they brought three pairs of sandals and water skins . . . they would need a camel or an ass to carry provisions . . . but there was no time for that . . .

Her mind whirled just as her body had danced so recently—but not in joy this time. She looked up at the brilliant blue-green bird in the cage, its throat chortling its beautiful but forlorn call. This was what she and Miriamne were and would become: prized possessions of a royal household, wives of men of high standing, not runaway adherents of prophets wandering in the desert calling out to all of Israel. Caged, treasured for their song, so long as the song was pleasing. Taken out of their impoundment at the behest of others to entertain and delight, then put back for most of their lives, rotting in a dry well as was John now. Perhaps it was better his life be ended quickly the way her mother wanted. She sank farther down the wall, letting her legs collapse indelicately, any concern for appearance gone. Her lips quivered and her breath came in short gasps as if she were squeezed by rocks like those piled on sinners to crush them to death. She would be confined for life—but she would never sing as sweetly as this bird, never dance again for the pleasure in her own heart, just to have it plucked from her like both of her parents were trying to do—her stepfather in his lasciviousness, her mother in her grasp for power, a mother who would appropriate every movement, every breath of life, every feeling that came out of her daughter if she could.

As Salomé lay there, the warm breeze stole down the hall and through the doorway, finding her in her stupor, as if any life were outside her and above her as she lay limp. The life that surrounded her was not the life she wanted—whether caged, like the birds, nor drunken, like Herod's guests, who were sated with wealth and lust and covetousness, nor clutching, like her mother, nor fearful like Miriamne. What was there in the world for her? Her heart and desires would have to become like Herod's great stone erections, his fortresses, to survive in such a world. Her mother's face rose up before her, spectral, driving her with a force she did not register in her body, propelling her seemingly dead limbs back out into the hallway. Nearly bumping into the servant Susanna who had offered to help her dress for the gala, she cried out.

"I beg your pardon, my lady. Is there anything I can get you?" the girl excused herself.

From somewhere in the depths of Salomé's mind a notion tugged at her. It was whispered, not spoken, so it wasn't clear, but she felt its lure and swung to follow it. Of course there had to be an escape that had not immediately occurred to her. With a conviction trying to gain its footing she said surreptitiously to the girl, "Go to the baths. I want you to tend to my mother and see that she does not leave for the banquet until . . . until . . . until after you have braided her hair in that new style you were showing me the other day and . . . and . . . bring her some new silk robes. Tell her there is a tear in the back of the one she is wearing. Tell her it's the wrong color. I don't care what you tell her, but keep her there as long as you can!"

The girl, bewildered, opened her mouth to question, but then clamped it shut. Salomé grasped her by the shoulders, turned her, and gave her a little shove in the direction of the baths. As the girl gave one last look back over her shoulder Salomé put her finger to her lips, pressing upon the girl that she was serious in her intent. The girl went soundlessly down the hall to her assignment.

Salomé moved through the corridors, passing a large courtyard filled with the heavy scent of some of her mother's fragrant transplanted bougainvillea. Hurrying past some guards, taking with her the stale hot air that had been circulating in the hallways, she moved out beyond the walls of the palace where the air expanded and mingled with the night sky in its own sea of warmth caressed by the surrounding purple and blue-shaded mountains. The bright moon one or two days off full silvered the landscape, bathing the desert as if it could also smooth the tight contractions of her heart that began to ripple through her chest.

A camel with fully laden saddlebags and water jugs stood tied outside the palace walls. Running her hand along its rough-furred side as she moved out into the night, Salomé found that being out in the free air, away from her mother, feeling the breathing animal under her hand, allowed her feelings to come alive. Surely she could find a solution by asking John. Or maybe she should simply take the camel and run away. She guessed that it belonged to Nattu, the captain of Herod's guard, but he was a good man; he wouldn't mind. She placed her cheek on the camel's musky hide near its rump. Then she arched her neck back to look at the moon. Slowly she raised her arms out to her sides at shoulder height, feeling a pull on either side, one by the moon glinting off the Dead Sea, the next by the alluring curves of the Moab hills receding into the dark. The swallowing cage of the fortress behind her nailed her to her spot, creating a crucifix of indecision. The tension of choice between her mother's affections and her sister's was too much for her young body to hold. Touching her tear-stained face, she looked down over the rampart and into the valley below to the shadows of the trash piles that had been doused from the day's burning. Yet the eerie night sky did not frighten her—on the contrary, it seemed as if it would soon speak its secrets, the secret to hers and Miriamne's true sovereignty over their own lives.

Knowing she had little time before her mother would go to the banquet hall and discover her daughter's absence, Salomé lashed herself forward. She had snuck out of the palace before, on one occasion at night, and found it quite thrilling, but tonight she felt much more was at stake; her fear was now a very real and large knot in the center of her chest. The consequences of getting caught this time would be severe, so she moved along quickly in the direction of the cistern, rolling over in her mind anxiously what she would say to John.

She looked down at the slippers on her feet, now dusty. Picking up one foot, she removed the shoe and shook a pebble out of it, and as she placed it back on her foot she suddenly ached with the realization that she was proposing to go seek out the very man whose head she had been told to request. How welcome had she thought she would be? Even her mother wouldn't have suspected such stupidity to come from her. Perhaps the camel had been placed there by God, by the man in the wilderness . . . she could take the camel and go find the man in the wilderness! The camel now seemed her only possible means of escape. Its bags were loaded; she could take it and survive for the number of days it would take her to locate the man . . .

Muted wailing reached her ears and her mind's whirling ceased. Looking down the rampart, in the sharply silhouetted sky she saw a tall, strapping man who looked to be Nattu, dragging what Salomé thought was Miriamne. Her sister was thrashing about, and Salomé could hear Nattu speaking to her in exasperation.

"Your Highness, forgive me, but the tetrarch has forbidden anyone to see the prophet John anymore. I'm only carrying out my orders."

"Why is it . . . Do you not have a heart? You have a woman—you know love—please just grant me this." Her cries were part way between a child's whine and those of a pitiful and desperate woman.

Salomé looked back at the camel, and then back at Nattu. The beast was his. He was, indeed, a good man, having been gentle with Salomé and Miriamne, and she knew the pagan woman with whom he had made his home these last several years from the market. She had a kind but plain face, and Salomé imagined that Nattu loved her for who she was to him rather than for her beauty. Salomé didn't want Nattu to suffer on her account. Her mother's desires pulsed at her back, in the palace, and her sister's pain tugged on her from the front. To the north, into the hills, was only a weak hope. Before Nattu and Miriamne had come close enough to see her, she let out all her breath, dropped her head, and turned to let her numb feet lead her back to the palace.

Back in the banquet hall, as she stood in the door she saw Herod laughing and slapping a dignitary from the north on his back, but the look on Salomé's sweet contorted face arrested him. He turned to her and gestured, his eyes turning to slits, his mouth set grimly as it did whenever he and Herodias argued. Meeting Salomé in the center of the room, he reached for her hand, and once again the onlookers grew quiet, as if someone, as in the bird room, had thrown large fabric covers over all the cages of all the pomped-up dignitaries in the room. Herod motioned for the music to stop.

"What troubles you my sweet? Have you decided what you shall ask of me? Everybody is waiting to hear." He half-smiled and cocked his ear toward her, speaking in the most gentle voice that was available to him.

The air was fetid and a smell of vomit reeked from a corner, mingling with the incense, as if someone had not made it out of the room in time. Servants stood, their countenances set, trained to ignore the indelicacies occurring around them that tended to happen at this late stage of a party. Salomé noticed that her stepfather looked more pig-like than ever, his slitted eyes in his fleshy face scanning her expression to determine what exactly it was she would ask of him. He reached out to her cheek a pudgy hand with long groomed fingernails and the golden ring of his office, but she turned instinctively away from his touch.

"So this is what it comes down to? This existence?" Her eyes locked onto his, suddenly awakened to the pain of her imminent request.

Looking at her blankly at first, Herod's recumbent obtuseness again veiled his response. Then, figuring it out, he ignored the stab of her comment and said, "I don't understand. You have come back. What is it that you want?" For just a moment Salomé thought she saw a solicitousness in the pig's eyes, but then it evaporated and her stepfather stood before her, rooted as ever.

She pressed the request from her lungs, all sense of hope gone. "I have no choice but to . . . I . . . ask . . . you, your Highness . . ." her eyes searching the room desperately for some alternative, "for . . . the . . ." and she cried out, "for the head of John the Baptist." Her hands flailed ineffectually at her side as she blurted her orders.

Any remaining drunkenness collapsed from Herod's face. Loutish but not stupid, he recognized the thinly veiled demand as coming from his wife.

Speechless, he turned from her, looking over his shoulder at the guests around his table, then the guests in another corner of the room. Those who had heard what Salomé called for were whispering to others the abomination, and all waited to see how Herod would respond; their twittering had resumed.

"Mmph." It was a grunt. He chewed his lip. Stalling, then quietly, so only Salomé could hear, he said, "Is this your mother's request." It was not so much a question as a statement, because he knew the answer.

She could only nod in anguish, her head turned aside in shame. Desperation seeped from her very being, the blue-green silk hanging limp about her now, the glittering belt lying dully on her dead hips. The room was leached of its color, the guests merging into a great amorphous glob. A boy, barely more than twelve, blonde-haired and beautiful, was fascinated with the hawk in the corner and was trying to feed it an olive. It jabbed at him, causing him to yelp. Only the few nearest heads turned. Crushed grapes underfoot made the floor slippery, and trays of picked-over food littered the tables. The musicians looked nervously back and forth from one another, their tune stilled and hanging on Herod's pleasure, but he was absorbed in searching his stepdaughter's face again.

"On a silver plate," Salomé whispered, not daring to look at Herod, though she felt him boring through her now cruelly, in anger, devoid of any lingering sexual urge. How quickly his push for power came to the forefront!

Herod turned, muttering to himself, "She might as well cut off my manhood from my body than John's head from his." Then, gathering himself like a lion rising out from a cave he lunged toward his stepdaughter and roared at her, "John is a prophet! A holy man! Cut off his head? Do you have any idea what his followers will say? This will start a war. Are you your mother's puppet?" Spittle at the corners of his mouth, he loomed over her as if he would swat. A deathly stillness sank on the room as people fully took in what Herodias had enjoined her daughter to do. Some of the women whispered to one another; the hawk in the corner raised its head off its breast, one eye open over its sharply curved beak.

Then they heard a shriek—not the bird, but Miriamne, having appeared again at the darkened door. She ran into the room, shoved Salomé, who staggered and fell, then threw herself at Herod's feet.

"Your Highness, I beg you, do not do this thing . . ." Miriamne sobbed. "My sister is out of her mind—she doesn't know what she's asking for—she's made up this request—our mother would never ask for such a thing . . . my sister is jealous of me," she wailed as she tugged at his tunic.

Herod, now truly confused as to why his other stepdaughter was so passionately pleading for the prophet's life, merely kicked her away from him and scowled down at her. As she groveled, Salomé came forward to take her by the arm to lift her up off the floor. But Miriamne pushed at her, and reeling away from both of them, sobbing, turned to run out of the room.

Light and moods played across Herod's face as it seemed to Salomé that his very being tried to encompass both hatred of his wife's manipulations as well as his lingering lust for his stepdaughter after her performance. She knew him to be good, when it came to ruling, at separating out competing issues and desires in his mind, but when such harshly opposing urges lay themselves out before him, demanding his response on the spot, he was taxed. He wavered on an edge, not sure if he should take the murderous plunge laid out before him.

The beating, blood-filled thing in the center of Salomé's chest contracted suddenly and sharply on seeing Miriamne's distress, and her love flew out to her sister. She followed her now, running out to seek her in the hallways, hands gathering her skirts.

"Miriamne! Miriamne! Come back. It's not about us . . ." Her words wafted on the currents of warm night air down the corridor, hollow. Her heart empty now as she turned about and did not find her sister, Salomé stood and contemplated her next move. Life swept up through her, rage flooding. Reentering the room, she brushed past a table, picked up a plate of olives, and flung it at Herod, who had his back to her. It hit him squarely on the left shoulder and splattered in an oily smear on his tunic. She lit toward him, clawing his back from his shoulders on down as he turned toward her. One of her nails had missed his shoulder and caught his cheek. Blood dotting his face, he reeled backwards as he put up his arms to protect himself even as she screeched at him, "You animal! You half-blooded bastard! I would sooner see you die!"

Face livid, she spewed guttural words as her lips curled back in a snarl at him. She spun around, searching for something else to throw at him, knowing at a condensed, animal level that the only way to empty her body of the cumulative unexpressed rage of her mother, her sister, her stepfather, at one another and at life, was to swing her arms and throw something, anything. Grabbing wine goblets, dishes, food, Salomé cleared off nearby tables as guests screamed and ducked. Herod retreated behind a table to escape an onslaught that was not just hers alone, then motioned to the captain of the guard and some nearby servants to subdue Salomé.

"Nattu!"

Getting pelted himself with whatever her fingers had found, Nattu, who had come in behind Miriamne, did as he understood Herod's meaning and ran over to Salomé, pinning her arms behind her back. A servant helped him as her knees buckled and she folded to the floor, her hair askew and her dress filthy now. The scarf lay in the center of the room, and as Nattu apologetically but swiftly bound her wrists with some cord, the servant went to retrieve the scarf for her.

Salomé lay, legs bent underneath her, panting in her spent rage. "I'm like Mumma, just like her. No different inside," she thought despairingly to herself, believing only that she had acted out her anger just as she had danced her joy a short while ago. At least she expressed it rather than hid it behind control and manipulation. She looked up at Nattu. He could not meet her eyes.

"You have made my decision for me," Herod said as he looked down on his stepdaughter. "Nattu."

Turning the distraught but no longer struggling girl over to a handful of servants nearby, the captain of the guard approached Herod as told, but warily. His arms bulging, veins rivering his forearms, he stood a good five inches taller than his ruler, dwarfing the tetrarch to comical effect.

Loud enough for most people within his range to hear, Herod declared, "I am a man of my word. I gave my word to you that I would grant you whatever you asked. You have asked. We must be careful what we wish for, no? Nattu, bring me the head of John the prophet. ON A SILVER PLATTER!" he yelled directly into the face of the captain.

Salomé curled into a squat on the floor, stunned and dumb, head bowed. Her rage had extinguished John's life. His death was her fault.

7

Night

THE ROOM had buzzed at various volumes for what seemed about another half hour, waiting for the gruesome outcome, to see if Nattu would return as ordered. Salomé, bound and still guarded, had been taken to the corner near the hawk, positioned almost underneath it, yet she was only fleetingly aware of its presence, so exhausted was she. It sat on its perch, keenly watching the commotion in the room, scanning, scanning to see if anything was available for eating. Its dark eyes glittered in the torchlight. Every so often it would pick up one leg, slowly uncurling its claw from the perch, then place it back down, ratcheting its knuckles to grip the wooden branch on which it balanced. It seemed to wait.

Salomé alternately wept and wiped her eyes on the back of her roped hands and carried out another internal dialogue as if it could shield her from the eyes of tens of people whose presence she had so recently judged. "I am shamed. These are my people, should be my people, but I'm foreign here. I don't belong with them. I can't ever live among them—but where can I go? Miriamne will hate me now. Mumma clearly doesn't want me, and I can't bear to be near Mumma," she thought. This death of affection was worse than stoning, she felt, as she stood alone in the corner. With more venom in her heart than she knew she had, she hated Herod—for shaming her, for using her like her mother had used her. But the terror of having opposed her mother fought in her heart as well. It was all too hard: within this

life of luxury, an existence for which she had so much to be grateful, she had only room for hate and burning fear that threatened
to slay any natural kindness in her. No wonder people masked
their faces and draped themselves in fine linens and hid behind
the numbing stupor of wine. No wonder they vacated their very
souls to vie for power. She would have to do the same.

Her childhood crushed, at that moment she looked up to see
Herodias enter the room through the door where Miriamne had
so recently stood. Looking condescendingly over at her bound
daughter, Herodias went and reclined next to Herod, fanning
out her dress and its layers behind her. The ruler and his wife did
not look at one another, and for a few minutes conversation in
the room rose to a higher nervous pitch than that at which it had
been percolating. Finally, Herodias spoke to her husband.

"How was the dance?"

He spun on his seat to face her. His face twitched.

"It was delightful. You missed a luscious performance. You
have trained your daughter well, and influenced me . . . again.
At your vengeful hand I have ruined your daughter's sweetness.
And we will go to war again; you'll see. I hope this is what you
wanted." He plastered a grin on his face at the end of his speech
to reassure anyone who might be looking that he was speaking
peaceably with his wife, then turned stiffly from her.

Herodias plucked a remaining grape from a stripped cluster. Holding it between her teeth, she bit down on it and closed
her lips to contain its spurt within her mouth. As she chewed she
likewise spread a false smile across her face.

"He is only a small prophet," she murmured, admitting
her husband's accusation. That they were discussing a man's
life seemed to slide past them as if they were reclining on the
banks of the Jordan itself, watching the water of John's life slip
downstream.

"And now it appears your other daughter, the weepy one,
has been in love with the man!" He was still turned from her.

"That has been her foolish preoccupation. I neither encouraged it nor discouraged it," Herodias responded. "I love both of my daughters, but I will not see them ruin themselves with lovesick desires and imprudent notions about men." Herodias ran her fingers over the wine-stained tablecloth in front of her and then dipped a piece of flat bread into some hummus. "Isn't this floral pottery from Jerusalem lovely?" she said in an effort to redirect her husband. He ignored her.

The music was playing again, and a few guests had wandered off, but most had remained, imbibing more, to see the end of the drama being played out before them.

Nattu had returned.

Herodias tilted her chin up and tapped her middle finger on the table impatiently, to see if what she had stipulated had been carried out.

The guard walked stiffly, shoulders squared, eyes straight ahead, as he entered and approached his master. He carried the requested silver platter gingerly. His oiled hair gleamed in the torchlight; his face was a study of composure to ensure he could carry out his nauseating task. Legs steady, about twelve feet in front of Herod and Herodias, he proffered the platter, now covered with a white cloth that showed some blood at its edges. With one deft movement he turned aside his head then whisked off the cloth to reveal the bloodied head of the prophet, dark dead eyes open and staring, it seemed, directly at Herodias. Sinews from his severed neck trailed on the platter, a pool of blood leaking at the base of the decapitation. Several loose strands of brown stringy hair clotted the collected fluids drained from vessels, sinuses, and spinal cord. Herodias stared back, only her own bloodless cheeks betraying any response.

Nattu spoke. "As you have ordered, my lord, the head of the prophet John."

A conclusive hush fell over the room. A small-boned young man vomited, and one of Herodias's woman friends fainted.

Herod had not looked, and now kept his head turned away in distaste; certainly, he had seen decapitation and dismemberment before in battle, but the contrast of the bloody scenario against the civility of the party shocked even his system. Herodias continued to stare at the head, eyes hard, with only a small working of her jaw that Salomé could see.

But before Salomé even had time for her own reaction, the hawk above her head screamed and flew up off its perch, straining against its leash. With one slicing jab at the thin leather restraining it, the bond broke and the bird lit across the room, swooping toward the platter in a fluster of brown and white feathers. It dove at the head, stabbing at the eyes, grappling with the nose and face first. Its claws dug into the eye sockets and it plunged in with its beak, wrestling for a black glittering orb to pull it out of the socket despite the ligaments still trying to hang on. Nattu stumbled and dropped the dish so that the bird, still clinging to the head to finish its task, scrabbled in a mass of bird feathers and human hair, flapping toward Herodias's and Herod's table, smearing blood mixed in with smashed grapes and humus all over the marble floor. Herod's face had gone white as he and Herodias dove forward, scattering food and plates about them, as the bird screeched one last time and rose in the air, successfully plucking the eyeball from the head and seeking an exit. Finding the corner door, it flew out and down the corridor with its prize.

8

Thirty-eight years later,
the ruins of Machaerus fortress, 67 CE

I HAD been sleeping better since I had begun working with the queen, and my dreams had been less agitated, more peaceful, as if I had become a part of the dream of her life while she recalled snippets of it for me, days running by in the composition of her narrative. On occasion she had talked about Herodias, which would leave me to think about my own mother as I wound my way home each day at the end of the writing employment. I recognized that by having gone to live in Jerusalem, apart from my family, I had begun to have inklings that my life would one day be my own when my mother was gone. Being back in Machaerus with my family for this time of writing underscored that fact, and while I could be taken with bouts of nostalgia, I was generally not sorry I had gone to live with my aunt and thus to befriend Nathaniel.

We had begun Salomé's narrative by addressing it to Theophile, the widow I had met the first day of the project. Thereafter the most memorable passages would often drift through my head at the end of the day. Though Salomé had frequently stressed that women were intellectual beings, with minds and hearts as great as men, more than just reproductive machines, I particularly liked the story she spun of the babe leaping in the womb of the woman named Elizabeth when her kinswoman Mary had come to visit. Because her husband Zechariah had been struck dumb by the angel Gabriel, she named the child John. It was only after Zechariah agreed to the name that he regained his speech. So each day had unfolded with more fascinating developments and characters whose actions often defied my belief.

"We must press forward. This clash between the Romans and Jews will destroy our history, I fear, if we do not preserve it. For today we shall talk about that fox, Herod. No—no, he was more a pig than a fox," Salomé began this morning. Salomé, who, since we had been working together for a while now, allowed me to address her with familiarity out of reach of Susanna's ears, rubbed her eyes as if to rid them of the day's haze and moisture. Burn piles from the valley below sent small odorous curls of blue-black smoke trailing into the Moab mountains. She tapped her fingers on the broad windowsill, thinking, then turned back to me.

"No doubt you would like to know more about him. He was my stepfather, of course. In some ways I can say nothing more about him; he silenced nearly everyone around him until he lost his mind with the quiet that pressed in upon him. He never experienced the silence as the presence of God—that I knew of, anyway. The only person he didn't silence was my mother; from what I have heard from those who saw out their last days with them in Gaul, she kept up a steady stream of influence into his ear and mind. Not that she could wield any power with it; they were stripped of any worldly power. Rome made sure of that."

I shifted minutely in my seat, which was a little small for my rear end, uncomfortable that Salomé was speaking more intimately of her past than she had to date. Hired as a scribe for her project, I had been steadfastly performing my duty, but she seemed to have warmed to me as she had built her narrative and I recorded it. Tucking my toes underneath me to align my spine and sit up straighter, I waited out the queen as she looked over the expanse toward the Dead Sea and continued in a dreamy voice, almost as if I weren't there in the present but rather back in the time of her youth.

"It wasn't that they left me alone when they took themselves off together after Rome increased its presence; they had taken their twosome and excluded the rest of us long before they ever left these lands. That twosome sustained them in a world unto themselves, no matter in which fortress or city they lived. Even when they hated each other they didn't want to let anyone else in, including Miriamne and me; they wanted their malice to themselves. Others who tried to encroach on that only infuriated her, and befuddled him. As far as I can discern, anyway. I understand that when they got to the end of their days in Gaul, both of them being stricken with the loss of mind that can come with old age, they grew softer toward one another—perhaps harkening back to their good early days together. Still, the paradise that such old age forgetfulness sometimes is, even then, did not include anyone else.

"Of course, she didn't exactly explain her anger, and, I believe, the fear that was underneath it, when others would insert themselves between them. She just took it out on the rest of us. I doubt she even knew she was so angry. She certainly wasn't very solicitous of how others felt, and for a very long time I couldn't decide if she even loved me, and Miriamne. I had darker wonderings, too . . ." she drifted off here, but then resumed, "It looked like love at times, which was what was so confusing. But . . . rather than love, like a viper she consumed everyone around her as if we were food. Yet we were all starved for affection, and so was she. This is how I make sense of it now." She turned a strange wry face to me momentarily, the fingers of her hands tapping together lightly.

"I was told that at the end, after she had fallen and broken her back on a set of stairs in Gaul, she vomited. The vomiting was the only sign her own body gave her that pain was present. She didn't feel."

I sat very still, uncomfortable with this level of intimacy I was being granted. Salomé's eyes looked far away now, out over the Dead Sea, her gnarled hands resting on the stone windowsill. Years of abstract cognition, or maturity, lay heavy on her shoulders, I thought, a mantle she would not have chosen (but how many of us invite it?). Now it pressed down so on her that she stooped and her back curved toward a hump. I often wondered if the layers of experience resting on old people were painful, and if, in Salomé's case, she missed the light freedom of dance from her earlier years. I wondered how long she had taken to gain resolution toward her mother; for that matter, how did anyone come to forgiveness? It was a question my young mind had circled around many times.

For now I paused in my writing, waiting. In the previous days and weeks we had been working on the project together I had gotten good at figuring out when I needed to write, and when not. Salomé was resolutely clear as to how she wanted her narrative to unfold. While my hands were grateful for the break now, I wanted to get back to my task, unsure how to respond appropriately to her divulgence. Impressive with her learning and exposure to different literatures, facile in Greek and Hebrew and Aramaic and Latin all at once, she had put to the test my education. Theater she loved, Euripides in particular, and I could see how such knowledge had influenced what we were writing. I did feel some ownership at this point—but my own contribution would never, could never, be known. I was to be a silent partner. Soon we would finish. Rarely had I spoken up, and only then to seek clarification about spelling or names.

Today, though, I felt as though she wanted me to question her, to engage her in pulling up memories, as if somehow I could witness to them and thereby purge her of them—though I was not sure how such memories would influence what we were working on. Perhaps that is the greatest gift we give one another: to listen. I was about to ask her the most insistent question that had come to my mind in recent weeks, especially in the wake of her talking now, but we were interrupted.

The young Joachim ran through the curtain and over to his grandma. She held his face in her two hands and smiled at him.

He had been followed by two servants, who carried between them an ornately decorated chest.

"Where shall we set this down for you, your Highness?" asked one of them. Taking her eyes, but not her hands, off Joachim only momentarily, Salomé nodded with her head to a spot just under the window on the west side that overlooked the burn piles and the sea. Silently bid in this manner, the men like ghosts did as they were instructed and left the room.

"What have you got for me today?" Salomé asked of her grandson.

"Only a lizard, granny," said the boy, biting his lip and tilting his head as a tiny green lizard emerged from his fist and scooted up his arm, then leapt onto Salomé's dress. Startled as if she were still a girl, she brushed off the reptile as it scuttled up her breast and onto her shoulder. Scraping it off too hastily, she sent the lizard sailing out the window. Joachim squealed, ran to the opening, and stood on tiptoe to look out down below as the fated lizard sashayed through the air and vanished out of sight as it neared the ground. Joachim began to cry, so Salomé stooped to pick him up and hold him to her.

"Darling, I'm so sorry—I was just surprised," she apologized. As he wailed into her shoulder she looked over at me, furrowing her brows and patting her grandson's back, bouncing him up and down. "Ah, the lives of the little ones we are to care for are so dear to us . . . I'm so sorry sweetheart. Let it go. I'll get you another one."

"I don't want another one—I want that one!" he yowled.

"Shhh, shhh," she comforted, and eventually, as I had begun to notice with distraught children, the crying stopped—as it always did. He had spent himself on the notion of the splattered reptile, and was ready to move on, apparently having forgiven his grandmother. She reached into a small silk pouch she had strung around her waist and pulled out a bright, shiny new coin and pressed it into his hand.

"Here—have a new coin from Egypt. Go show it to your sister and then tell her to come see me."

Absorbed in the unusual design of the burnished money, wiping his nose on his arm, he slid down from Salomé's grasp and ran out of the room. As she stood, she ran her fingers over the trunk before her, then turned back to me.

"Now, where were we?"

"You were speaking of your mother, your Highness. I . . ."

"I was going . . . I'm sorry, I interrupted you," she said as she had begun speaking before I finished getting my words out. Never had I spoken with someone so considerate of others in conversation.

"I just—I just wondered . . . I don't know how to put it," I said, my impertinence rising up before me and threatening to suck back in my words.

"It's all right. Ask."

"I wonder how you forgave her, that's all. I mean, you seem to have. Perhaps I presume too much—but unforgiving people always strike me as angry, and you don't seem angry as you speak of her. Your description is complicated—but you don't sound angry. Angry people also make a lot of noise about how they're not angry anymore—beating their own breasts, sort of. At least that's what I've noticed. Not that I've had a lot of experience with it," I trailed off lamely in my uncertainty.

"You're astute for your young age. What I have found is that forgiveness works in a spiral." Here she wound her finger in circles near her head, and laughed a little at the implication.

Just then Meira came running into the room and gave us a new interruption. The queen's face lit up in delight but as she bent down with her arms extended for her granddaughter this time she winced. Meira stopped short, having seen both the circular motion Salomé made about her head as well as the look of pain on the woman's face.

"Granny, are you okay today?"

"Fine, dear, just fine. Sweet heart, there's something I want you to do for me when you are a bit older. You see this nice young woman here? She's writing down some things that are very important to me. To many people. And you know Theophile, the . . ."

"The dark, scary lady in the black?"

"Well, yes, dear, though she's really not so scary—just sad. What I want you to do when you are a bit older and have increased in your learning is to help Theophile make sure that the document this nice young woman here is writing, which belongs to you and Theophile and all of us, gets to a certain bookbinder. I will leave you instructions . . ."

"Can't you just tell me, Granny?"

"Not really, darling. I thought I would write it down for you in case we are in different places when you're older. I expect that, like your Granny, you will travel to many places throughout your life, maybe even going across the sea."

"I always want to see you, Granny."

"And so you shall. Now go back and find your brother," the queen said, and Meira went out of the room as happily as she had come in, thus commissioned.

Salomé resumed what she had been telling me. "You know that the authors using the pseudonyms of Mark and Matthew detail the prophet Yeshua talking about forgiveness; we've talked at length in the preceding weeks about their accounts of Yeshua's story. Incidentally, we will call our narrative the "Gospel of Luke.""

Hastily I wrote this down.

"I'll explain later why I am choosing a man's name, and we will have a second part to it to write after we are done with this one, so you'll be employed for a while longer yet. Being lettered as you are, you will probably recognize I'm drawing on many sources for my story. Now, back to what I was saying. You also know we are taught that forgiveness should occur when someone first wrongs you, then comes to make recompense, whether through words or money, as in paying off a debt. The formula is certain, determined, and very, very old, dating back to our most cherished sages."

I nodded my head in assent, curious about the lesson but holding myself very still, very quiet, so that she would not be distracted. I only hoped we would have no more distractions from outside the room. It seemed the words were coming directly from a deep well of heart and mind within her, and now I wanted her to know I was listening as if my life would never be the same. The heat blew into the window in pockets, bathing us both, as she stood and looked out the window and spoke with her back to me.

"Yeshua taught something different. It was so difficult! As I mentioned once before, I think, after my mother accomplished her abomination of having John killed, I did run away, and I joined the group of women who followed Yeshua. You see, it wasn't just John's head she had severed; she cut off any hope of closeness I could have had with her. So I took my life into my own hands rather than leave it in hers. It might not have turned out so well had I left my fate to her." She turned to smile at me, and I waited.

"But as Lamentations tells us, the wilderness is a sword, and it pierced my girlish notions of love for Yeshua as a man. I became content to understand him as he meant all of us to adhere to him, and I also gained my first experience of family by joining the group of Yeshua-followers. You know how they say that we have to be careful of what we wish for—it's so true. You may wish for one thing, but have no concept of the trials you'll be put through to arrive at the very thing you desired. Anyway, it took me a very long time to forgive my mother, but I learned how to do that after being in Yeshua's presence for the length of time I was."

I couldn't contain myself any longer and blurted out, "But how can you forgive someone who never asked your forgiveness?" Clapping my hand over my mouth, I saw her eyes move from the faraway look to hone in on me and my question in the present. Thankfully, I had not destroyed the moment of stillness that lay in her heart; she continued, able to track my urge to know.

"Because I saw him forgive the day they strung him up. He knew that forgiveness could, and needed to, be given even if someone—all of us—had never asked him for forgiveness. The people who put him on the cross bars never asked him to forgive them! Yet he could grant it. Even more than John. Thank heavens they took him down before the dogs began eating him, as they did the other two men who hung alongside him," and I could see her go off into the land behind her eyes, a grim look on her face, recalling the day of Yeshua's death. I didn't care to ask her to fill in the details; I had seen enough of the bloody and strangling torture that was crucifixion, and had heard enough of the particular tale of Yeshua's death. The death itself was no more extraordinary than any others who died in that manner, of that I was certain.

"But your question is a good one." She moved about the room, running her fingers over the bed frame, then the branches on the succulents, then the windowsill. "We are told again and again that we should forgive. As you and I have written down, we are to love our enemies, just as God is kind to the ungrateful and the selfish. And even to the one who handed him over, I believe. At no point, no matter how unforgiving I felt toward my mother, did God stop loving her. Yeshua was clear: forgive, and God will forgive you. So I knew God would forgive me my bitterness, my hatred toward my own mother, my wish at times that she would die. Wishing your own mother would die! Not because she was in pain . . . but because I wanted to claw the last traces of her out of my skin and bones. I realized one day I was in peril because the measure I was giving was the measure I was, and would be, getting back. You know: what goes around comes around, as the young people say now. Unforgiving people don't end up receiving the love of God in their hearts. Now, John emphasized repentance in his way: repent, forgive, or else—at least, that's how I saw it—but Yeshua's voice was different—as if he would press you through the very heart of God like love through a sieve and bring you closer to God because you would truly feel what it felt like to be forgiven, to have that close turn of your face back to God . . . well, when you did that, you couldn't help but give the same back to everyone in your life.

"John did what he could while he was here. But in the end he could only point the direction to Yeshua, wandering in the silence out there"—she looked out over the Moab hills turning their lavender gray shade in the early afternoon dust—"I never did understand why Miriamne loved John so, what she saw in him. Except that she was as starved for love as was I."

After a moment of contemplation, she continued. "Still, you know, precisely how to arrive at that forgiveness is very hard. I see this even now as those of us calling ourselves Christians go about proclaiming the new way." She turned to me and in exasperation continued, "In the prayer the Lord left us, that you wrote down for me, you see that he says 'Adonai, forgive us our human sins against You in the same way that we forgive the debts others hold with us.' Yet no instructions accompany how to do this! And when you can't repent or make amends by giving turtledoves to the priests, or when the person who has wronged you never even asks to come back into community with you, how are you supposed to forgive? What if there is no repentance forthcoming from the person at whom you are so angry? And even if you forgive a person when that person hasn't asked you to do so, doesn't that make you look a little like you're trying to be God, or the Son of Man?" Her words poured out like hot pressing lava covering any thought or comment I might have.

"We are instructed that we should forgive—but we are not taught how to. It's so very simple, but so very difficult. It was Yeshua's grace that taught me. First you must acknowledge that you have been wronged. For years I was too proud to admit this, as if I were somehow weak by the admission, as if Herodias had all the power to hurt—and I had none of the power. But then, after she died, I was so weary of the stone of anger pressing down on my heart that I decided I needed to let it go. That stone was her weight, not mine. Or, it was more like her poison. I suppose it's easier to let go if someone's dead, but it's still possible if the person is alive, even around you. I've seen it.

"I spent a few months in solitude one year, after I had moved to the north and married my second husband, Aristobulus, and we had our three boys. One day I realized that I could never understand completely what their lives would be like—particularly after I would be gone!—and so I shifted that understanding to the knowledge that, just as with my children, I couldn't see my mother from all sides. I have seen some evil in my life, and one thing I have noticed about its nature is that it is fundamentally confusing. There were times when I could not decide if my mother were evil, or if she loved me. Can you imagine that? I don't suppose you can. Such a bewildering thing for a young mind! To wonder if the woman who bore you is evil. But I didn't know her when she was younger; I didn't know what had happened to her to make her so frightened, so blindly grasping for love herself, mixing up love with power in the process. And if she had been alive, I realized it didn't mean I would have tolerated her treatment of me anymore; she was in many ways an . . . unlikeable . . . woman. Even now I'll stand by that. I didn't excuse her conduct, for her manipulating me to call for John's death. But I changed the way I thought about why she did those things. Do you know what happened?" Her ardor cooled as she questioned me softly but penetratingly. "In making that shift inside I gained a power greater than my mother had ever known or would have known what to do with if it had fallen at her feet like a starling out of the sky."

My face rapt, tears began at the corners of my eyes. "Then are you never . . ." I groped for the idea.

"There's one final piece. Let me just finish. Had I never known the deprivation of love from her, and had her bitterness turned me from her, I would never have turned around to find the love of Yeshua, Adonai, my sons, Aristobulus. And my grandchildren, Meira and Joachim, whose acquaintance you have made. Never would I have had the love their lives bring me. My mother served me a platter of fury and neglect—and horror, as her actions attest. Yet in that lack—probably especially because of it—I sought nourishment. If a person looks hard enough she can find love in the driest of places." Here Salomé again looked out to the desert. "My mother could have done the same for herself if she had looked. Now, what were you going to ask?" Her face beaming, she turned to face me, then walked over to the chest the men had brought in and ran her hands over it.

It took me a minute to let her words sink in. I opened my mouth, but nothing came out.

"As relates to the death of John, Mark and Matthew cover my story adequately in their narratives. We will not address it in this one." I could not see her face now, but would have liked to.

Finally I found my voice. "Do you never have anger toward your mother, then? Have you completely forgiven?"

Salomé looked over her shoulder at me, smiled a sad half smile. "What do you think?" She opened the trunk. An old and diminished but still foul odor emanated from the intricately carved interior. I stood to crane my neck and peer into the box, and recoiled with a whimper as I saw the skull of a man nestled in swaths of green and blue silk, along with some locks of perfectly preserved brown, curled hair. Cavernous sockets sank in where the living eyes had looked out. Slowly, reverently, Salomé picked up the skull, her aged hands caressing its cool roundness. She turned the skull to face me, holding it out, and said, "My mother's final gift to me before she died. The memory of John. What do you think she intended?"

She lifted the skull a little higher and with it floated to the window.

"I loved her, you know," she said, and she reached her arms up and out, the sleeves of her cloak pulling up. Swinging, her arms sent the skull spiraling out and down to join Joachim's lizard and the burn piles in the valley.